Mike yawne
post from the
me?" he wondered as he tore the brown
envelope open. Inside, there were two tickets
which he pulled out; it took a moment to
register.

"THE DEAD ZOMBIES!" he shouted out,
punching his fist in the air. "I don't believe it.
Two tickets for the Dead Zombies concert.
That's fantastic!"

The Zombies were riding high in the charts
and at the moment they were really hot. He
looked again inside the envelope, but there was
no letter or note to indicate who might have
sent the tickets.

"This is crazy. Cool, but crazy," he muttered
to himself, turning the envelope over in his
hand. He hoped that he might recognise the
handwriting, but the address had been typed.

"I don't know who my fairy godmother is
but it must be someone who knows me," he
thought, looking towards his collection of
CDs and tapes. He had every one of the
Zombies' albums and was saving up for their
next release.

"When is this concert?" he said aloud,
picking up the tickets from the table.
"September fifteenth at the Queen's Stadium.

"That's tomorrow. This is too good to be true!"

He picked up the phone and was just about to call his best friend Steve with the good news when he had second thoughts.

"If I tell Steve that I've got some tickets for the concert, then the first thing he's going to do is ask me if he can come along... I've got a better idea. Yes, a much better idea."

He sprang off the sofa, opened the door and bounded up the stairs two at a time to his bedroom. From the bedside cabinet, he picked up his address book and thumbed through until he found the name he was looking for. "Rachael Astley," he mused to himself, as he thought of her long, flowing, auburn hair and lovely smile. She was a girl from his year group at school. He had known her for a long time. They had always been friendly but over the last few months he had found himself strangely attracted, even fascinated by her. He often discovered himself stealing a secret, sideways glance at her in class and wondered if he had the nerve to ask her for a date. If he didn't do it soon, then he was sure that someone else would. She was the kind of girl any guy would like to date.

Apart from his natural shyness, money had also been a problem; a night out on the town was costly and from what he knew of Rachael, she had expensive tastes. She always dressed well, usually wearing the latest style or some eye-catching piece of jewellery.

The money he earned from his Saturday job had to be spread very thinly; there was always the next Dead Zombies album to save for, and then there were nights at the bowling alley with his friends - but the tickets gave him a golden opportunity that he just couldn't ignore.

He dialled the number and waited. The phone rang several times before someone answered. From the sound of the voice, he guessed it was Rachael's mother.

"Hello, my name's Mike Campbell. Could I speak to Rachael, please?"

"It's for you, Rachael. Says his name is Mike," he heard her mother calling.

"Oh." He could just hear Rachael's surprised response and he began to wonder if he hadn't made a serious mistake.

"Yes?" she said, hesitantly.

He took a deep breath. "Rachael, I've got two tickets for the Zombies concert tomorrow and I was wondering if you'd like to come with me." That was all he was able to say as his tongue went dry and seemed to stick to the roof of his mouth. He waited for a response, screwing his face up as if he was about to receive a blow to the head.

There was a squeal of delight on the other end of the phone. "Of course I would!" she said with an enthusiasm which he hadn't been expecting. "I think their music is fantastic."

Mike felt himself blushing a bright red and was glad that no one could see him. "I'll be able to borrow my dad's car so I'll pick you up around seven thirty tomorrow evening. Is that all right?"

"I look forward to it. I'll see you tomorrow."

He put the phone down with a sigh of relief.

"Yippee!" he shouted as he jumped high and smacked his hand against the ceiling. He fell to his bed with a crash. "Dead Zombies, here we come!"

"What's going on up there?" he heard his mother shouting.

He didn't reply; he was already tapping out the phone number of his best friend, Steve.

"Steve, you'll never guess - "

"You've won the National Lottery," butted in Steve before Mike could say any more.

"I've finally cracked it."

"You've made an omelette then - big deal," quipped Steve, confirming his reputation for being a bit of a smart alec.

"I'm taking Rachael Astley to see the Dead Zombies tomorrow at the stadium."

There was a long whistle down the phone. "You lucky so-and-so. Wait till I tell the guys. They'll be green with envy. How did you manage to afford the tickets? They're selling for twenty-five pounds each!"

"They just came through the post today. I haven't got a clue who sent them to me, but I'm not complaining. At first, I thought the postman had made a mistake, but my name was on the envelope."

"I wish they had sent them to me," Steve complained. "Anyhow, it's great news but I'm sorry I can't stay talking to you, I've got an essay to finish for tomorrow. Enjoy yourself," he said, obviously wanting to bring the conversation to an end.

"Don't you worry about that, I will," said Mike, and hung up.

It was nine o'clock the next morning and Mike realised that he hadn't cleared it with his dad about borrowing the car for the evening. It was only a few weeks since he'd passed his driving test. He knew his dad wouldn't be too keen about lending his B.M.W. to number one son.

"Dad."

Mr Campbell looked up slowly from his newspaper. Mike knew instantly that his dad was going to exact a high price for the favour he was about to ask.

"Alright, what do you want?" Mr Campbell had heard that tone of voice before and knew what to expect.

"Can I borrow the car this evening? It's really important." It was the first time he'd asked and he was praying his dad would agree.

"I was wondering how soon you'd get round to borrowing the car. You can have it, but only on the condition that you give it a full valeting before you go. It's got to sparkle inside and out or the deal's off," threatened his dad, reluctantly sliding the keys across the table.

"At least it might do something for my image, to arrive in a shiny B.M.W.," Mike thought, as he took out the bowl and a large sponge from the cupboard.

By six-thirty Mike was as clean as the B.M.W. he had spent all morning polishing. For the last half hour he had been in the shower and was now standing in front of the mirror putting the final touches to his greatest asset - his jet black hair. He combed in every direction until he had it just right.

"Perfect," he grinned, giving a final once-over with his sister's hairspray to make sure it stayed that way.

"Style, that's what it's all about," he said, smoothing back his hair with his free hand as he gunned the B.M.W. out onto the road and burned rubber, much to the annoyance of his father.

Within ten minutes he had arrived outside

8

Rachael's house and, as he pulled to a halt by the driveway, he saw the front door opening. He took a deep breath and nervously drummed his fingers on the steering wheel. She closed the door behind her and walked up to the car with her freshly-washed hair blowing gently in the evening breeze.

"Wow! Step this way, Princess," he said, leaning over to open the door. He was a little apprehensive and he had decided beforehand that a bit of humour would help to break the ice.

She sat down carefully, adjusted her dress and smiled. "What are you waiting for? Let's go."

He raised his eyebrows in mock surprise then let the clutch out, pinning both of them into the padded leather seats as they accelerated down the road.

It was about half an hour's run to the stadium where the band were playing and he wanted to enjoy every minute of the journey. Rachael opened her purse and took out a Zombies cassette which she pushed into the tape player.

"Great music," he said, slowing down so he could give more attention to his passenger.

Mike turned off the dual carriageway and onto a country lane which he knew was a short cut into town. Ahead of them in the fading light there was a bridge. Mike reduced his speed as the road became narrower. They were travelling at about thirty miles an hour.

"There's someone on the bridge," Rachael

casually noted.

They drew closer. Mike shielded his eyes against the bright evening sky to get a better view. "It's probably one of the locals out for an evening stroll."

"It looks as if he's watching rather than walking," said Rachael with a slight sense of unease which she couldn't explain. The hairs on the back of her neck tingled inexplicably as the car drew closer to the bridge.

Mike felt a strong urge to look up again as he noticed a slight tremble in Rachael's voice, but as the lane was narrow and they were now approaching the bridge pillars, he had to keep his eyes fixed on the white line ahead.

"He seems to be holding something in his hands." Against the darkening sky she could see quite clearly the silhouetted figure of the man. "That's weird," she continued, straining her eyes to see more detail. It looked like a bundle of clothes or a bag, but she wasn't sure. "He's lifting it, over his head."

They were now only yards from the bridge and Rachael finally realised what it was. Her worst fears were confirmed and she screamed out in a terrified voice. "He's got a rock in his hands. Oh no! He's going to throw it at us! We're going to die!"

Chapter 2
THE HANGING MAN

Mike looked up in horror as the man on the bridge hurled the rock directly at them. Everything seemed to happen in slow motion as the object came hurtling down. There was a loud metallic bang as a large slab of concrete hit the front of the bonnet, bounced off and came up towards the windscreen. Mike reacted instinctively, slamming the brakes on as hard as he could. The tyres screeched as the car slewed to one side in half a circle. His hands gripped the steering wheel; the car juddered to a halt. He sat still for a moment in a state of shock, not moving, just thankful he was still alive. The concrete had just glanced off the edge of the windscreen causing a long fracture, but at least it hadn't smashed through.

He leaned over towards Rachael, who had her head pressed into her hands. "Are you alright?" he asked, reaching over and putting his arm around her. She nodded without saying a word.

Suddenly Mike, overwhelmed by a great sense of anger, jumped out of the car and looked along the top of the bridge. He just caught sight of a shadowy figure disappearing into the gathering gloom. Driven by fury, he sprinted up the grassy bank which led to the top of the bridge and began running at a frantic pace in the direction the attacker had taken. He turned left to follow the road and ahead of him he could see an eerie figure. He raced after him as fast as he could and within a couple of seconds realised that he was gaining ground.

The running man, who was now only thirty yards away, turned off the path and plunged into the deep undergrowth. Within a few seconds, Mike reached the spot where he had disappeared and was about to chase after him when he halted abruptly. He stopped and listened; he expected to hear a lot of noise as the man fought his way in the dark through the thick undergrowth, but there was no sound except the occasional hoot of a night owl.

"What am I doing?" thought Mike, as his heart pounded in his chest. "Suppose I catch him; he might have a knife; he might be a drug-crazed addict or a psycho who'll attack if he's cornered."

Mike listened again. He could hear the rustling branches swaying gently in the breeze. Then he thought he caught the sound of slow, heavy breathing. "He's in there, waiting for me."

The initial burst of adrenalin which had sent him chasing after his attacker was now subsiding. He felt suddenly afraid of the possibility that some demented creature was waiting for him to step foot into the undergrowth.

He spun round and hurriedly made his way back to the car, turning every now and then to make sure he wasn't being followed.

He found Rachael examining a large dent in the bonnet.

"The windscreen's cracked as well, but at least it didn't shatter," she commented.

Mike stared at the damage. "My dad is going to go ballistic when he sees what's happened to his car. It will cost a fortune to repair."

"Is that all you're bothered about?" said Rachael, with a hint of annoyance in her voice.

"I'm sorry, I wasn't thinking," apologised Mike, realising that he appeared more concerned with the state of the car than that of his passenger.

He put his arm around Rachael and brushed away a strand of her hair that had fallen in front of her eyes.

"How are you feeling?" he asked softly, trying to sound as sympathetic as he could.

"A bit shaky at the knees," she answered, happy that he was finally paying her some attention. "I'm just relieved that we've escaped uninjured. We could have been killed if that concrete had come straight through the windscreen. Why would anyone do such a thing? It's monstrous."

"It will be one of the local yobbos thinking he's being funny. Last week, a train was almost derailed when some idiot placed a railway sleeper on the track. That was only a few miles away from here."

"It's strange though," said Rachael, looking

around at the gathering shadows. "There aren't any houses around here. We're in the middle of the countryside. Why would someone be hanging around in this place?"

"I wish I could have caught him; I'd have given him more than a piece of my mind," said Mike, hoping he would impress Rachael. He didn't tell her that he had suddenly got very frightened and had given up the chase.

"It was rather brave of you," she said rising to the bait. "Or reckless. What would you have done if you'd caught him?"

Mike said nothing, preferring not to think about the possibility. He picked up the piece of concrete that was lying in the road and was just about to throw it into the ditch when he saw that there was something scratched onto it. He placed it in front of the car headlamp and his eyes opened wide as he saw the word 'DIE,' scrawled across the surface.

"Can you believe that?" he said, showing it to Rachael.

"Get rid of it," she said. "Let's get out of here, this place gives me the creeps."

Mike looked at his watch. "Do you still want to carry on? We've got time to get there if we hurry."

"Of course I do," she said, smiling and giving his hand a squeeze. "Let's try to forget about what's happened and enjoy the rest of the evening."

Fifteen minutes later they had arrived in

town, parked the car and joined the queue outside the stadium.

There was an air of excitement and anticipation as the waiting crowds were ushered through the gates into the main arena.

Mike tried hard to forget the incident, but it kept creeping back into his mind. What would have happened if the slab had gone through the windscreen? He was also worried about what his father's reaction would be when he saw the damage to the car.

"Tickets please," said the man at the gate.

Mike reached into his pocket for his wallet, took out the tickets and handed them over.

He watched as the ticket collector placed them under an ultraviolet light. The man turned to a colleague who was standing next to him, pointed towards the tickets then turned back to Mike.

"These tickets are forgeries. Where did you get them?"

He was just about to tell him they had been sent anonymously through the post, but he thought that would sound stupid.

"I bought them from a man in the street."

"Well, I'm afraid I can't let you in." He handed the tickets back to Mike and turned towards the next person in the queue.

"I can't believe it. What an absolute pain." He paused for a moment. "Now what do we do?" he said, turning towards Rachael. "Do you want to try somewhere else?"

"Let's go home," she suggested despondently. "This has really put a damper on the evening. I was really looking forward to watching the group."

"What a disaster," thought Mike to himself as he started the engine and began the journey home. A mile down the road, he indicated to turn right.

"You're not taking the same route back, are you?" said Rachael, startled as she realised what he was doing.

"It's twenty minutes quicker if we go this way. Surely, it's unlikely that we'll be ambushed again? Lightning doesn't strike twice in the same place."

Rachael was annoyed but said nothing. In the distance she could already see the bridge looming out of the darkness.

Mike, who had been showing a bit of bravado by pretending he wasn't frightened, suddenly thought he saw a figure on the bridge. In a panic, he put his foot down on the accelerator and the car surged forward; he closed his eyes and ducked instinctively as he passed underneath, half expecting something to come flying through the windscreen. Looking back in the rear view mirror, he realised that what he had thought to be a figure was just the moonlight shining on the raised parapet of the bridge. He breathed a sigh of relief.

"So much for macho man," said Rachael sarcastically, keeping her eyes fixed in front of her. She knew exactly what he was up to, trying to impress her.

Mike felt a bit embarrassed but said nothing.

Ten minutes later they stopped outside Mike's house. "Would you like to come in for a few minutes and have a cup of coffee before I take you home? There's no one in at the moment."

She turned to answer him, but then caught sight of something which terrified her.

Her face twisted with fear and she began to scream as she stared at the manifestation that she could see over his shoulder. Mike spun round and looked towards his house. His bedroom light was on and the curtains were wide open.

He breathed in sharply as he saw a sight that appalled him. Hanging from the light cable in his bedroom was a body which was swinging slowly from side to side.

Chapter 3
THE JOKER

Mike started to say something but he was so shocked the words came out all mixed up. He ran towards the house and began banging on the door as loudly as he could, until he remembered that there was no one in. He fumbled in his pocket for his keys, and, with some difficulty, finally opened the door. His hands were shaking as he grabbed the banister and bolted up the stairs as fast as he could, intending to run straight into the room.

As he reached the top step, he heard a click. The light had been switched off.

"Someone is still in the room," he whispered to himself. A cold tingle of fear rippled down his spine. He began to think of the awful possibility that the person who had thrown the concrete slab from the bridge had somehow got back to his house and was now waiting for him in the darkened room.

The same feeling of dread that had caused him to chicken out when he was chasing his attacker, crept over him like a black cloud.

"Mike?" came a voice from the bottom of the stairs. It was Rachael. She'd come in through the open front door. "Have you looked inside the room?"

"Not yet," he answered, thinking that his heart would burst out of his chest, it was

0

beating so fast. He felt like running away as he had done before, but how could he run away from his own house? Rachael was watching. She would think that he was a coward if he didn't do something.

"There's someone inside the room," he whispered. "I saw the light go off."

"Come down and we'll call the police," she urged.

Mike didn't hear her. He pushed the bedroom door open slightly, hoping he would be able to see without having to go in. The room wasn't completely dark; the light from a street lamp shone in. Through the crack in the door, he could see the figure hanging from the light cable. It was still swinging slightly, to and fro. He felt sick. The hanging man scared him, but even worse was the knowledge that there could be a murderer hiding in the room.

He looked around for something he could use to defend himself. He picked up his cricket bat which was leaning against the wall, and held it tightly in his hand while he tried to decide what to do. Should he charge in shouting and screaming, or creep in slowly, hoping to take whoever was hiding in there by surprise?

Clutching the bat in his right hand, he pushed the door open wider and stopped to listen. Apart from the thump of his own heart, there was silence. He felt along the wall until he found the light switch which he clicked back on. The blood drained away from his face as he looked at the hanging man. He couldn't see its features because the body was turned away from him.

Looking round the room, he expected to come face to face with the perpetrator of this awful crime but, to his amazement, there was no one there. The window was opened and he went over to look, thinking the murderer might have climbed out that way. He couldn't see anything because it was very dark. Someone could be hiding in the bushes.

Suddenly, there was a loud bang which seemed to come from inside the wardrobe. His heart missed a beat as he realised that there must be someone hiding there. He crept over, as quiet as a cat, with his bat raised above his head.

Reaching the wardrobe, he was about to pull the handle when the door burst open and a figure leapt towards him.

"Surprise, surprise! Scared you didn't I?"

Mike stared at Kate, his younger sister, in disbelief. "You stupid idiot! How low can you stoop, trying to frighten me like that with some cheap trick!"

"Trying to frighten you?" she said, with smug satisfaction. "You were scared out of your wits. Look at your face, it's as white as a sheet."

Mike went over to the thing which was

hanging from the light flex and spun it round.

"Wait till I tell dad that you've been stuffing pillows inside his best suit! You won't be so chirpy then!"

"You're a bit touchy, aren't you? It was only a joke."

Mike pulled a chair over and climbed up to untie the swinging effigy. It dropped down in a crumpled heap onto the floor. Mike picked up the tangled mess and threw it at his sister.

"Now put this lot back, and keep out of my room. I don't want to see you in here again."

"That was a rather childish trick to play," said a softly spoken voice.

"And who are you?" said Kate, turning round to see that there was someone standing in the bedroom doorway.

"This is Rachael," said Mike, embarrassed by the whole episode.

"So, this is your new girlfriend. The one you've been bragging to all your friends about. Well I hope she has more of a sense of humour than you have," said Kate, as she tossed her head of red curls and stormed out of the room, pushing past Rachael.

Mike led Rachael downstairs and into the living room. "Would you like a cup of coffee?" he asked sheepishly.

"I want to go home," she replied, with a sad look in her eye.

☠

Within ten minutes Mike brought the B.M.W. to a gentle halt outside Rachael's house.

"I'm sorry things worked out the way they did," he said, half hoping that he could retrieve something from the awful evening.

"So am I," cried Rachael, before he could say any more. "It's been a disaster from start to finish. And that stupid sister of yours seems to have a screw loose." She stabbed at the tape player and ejected the Zombies cassette, putting it carefully into her purse.

"It's now or never," thought Mike, as he gently leaned over towards Rachael.

"Don't bother," she said, edging out of his reach and opening the car door. "I can see myself in, thank you!"

She slammed the door and walked up the path to the house without even looking back.

By the time Mike arrived home, he was angry and ready to blame his sister for everything that had gone wrong that evening. He was just about to open the living room door, ready for a full blown argument when a thought occurred to him.

He really wanted to see Rachael again and it seemed like a good idea to get Kate on his side rather than against him. She could sometimes be extremely obstructive but, when she wanted, she could also be quite co-operative. She had already annoyed Rachael and he didn't want that to happen again.

He took a deep breath and entered the room in a different frame of mind. She heard him come in but didn't turn round.

"Kate?" he said, in a friendly manner. "Kate, I'm sorry I called you those names tonight, but that was the second fright I've had this evening."

When she heard what had happened, she began to sympathize with him, knowing what her father's reaction would be when he found out about the damaged car.

"Sit down," she said, as he finished the story. "You must be all shaken up. I'll make us some coffee and toast."

As she went into the kitchen, Mike heard the phone ring. He could hear Kate pick it up and begin talking. Ten minutes later, she was still there.

"So much for my coffee and toast," he mumbled under his breath. "I'm off to bed."

He lay on top of his duvet, thinking about the missed opportunities of the evening.

"I'll give Steve a ring when Kate has finished on the phone," he decided, yawning. "I need to talk to somebody."

He must have fallen asleep because he woke

later with a start. The phone was ringing downstairs. "Kate will answer that," he thought to himself as he glanced at the clock. "One o'clock!" he said, sitting up quickly. "Who could be ringing at this time of night?"

He struggled out of bed and made his way downstairs, hoping that the phone wouldn't stop ringing before he got there.

"Hello?" he said, as he picked up the receiver. There was no answer. "Who's there?"

He listened carefully. The line was obviously open but whoever was on the other end wasn't speaking. Mike decided to say nothing, but just listened.

Suddenly, a rasping, scratchy voice crackled down the phone, making Mike jump with fright. "You were lucky tonight. Very lucky. I almost got you. Next time you're going to DIE." This was followed by a long hysterical laugh, then the line went dead.

Chapter 4
COUSIN ANGELA

Mike stood rooted to the spot, not knowing what to do. His parents hadn't come in yet and his sister was fast asleep.

"It could be a crank call," he muttered to himself, but the fact that the caller had referred to the incident that had happened earlier in the evening made this unlikely. He shuddered to think that someone might actually be prepared to kill him.

As he turned to leave the room, the phone rang again. His stomach churned over with fear. Surely the same person wouldn't be ringing back, but who else would be calling at one o'clock in the morning? He thought for a moment, then decided to answer it. This time he said nothing but just listened.

"Is that you Mike?" asked a voice that he didn't recognise. "Don't you know me? I didn't scare you too much with that phone call, did I?" said the giggling female on the other end of the phone.

"Who is it?" replied Mike, half angry and half relieved.

"It's Angela, your cousin. Don't you remember me? We've just moved back into the area."

"Remember? How could I forget?"

Angela had lived in the same street as Mike

five years ago, before her family had moved to a different part of the country. She and Kate had been good friends then, and had thought it hugely funny to play tricks on him. Angela's leaving present had been a live frog in his lunch-box, which had caused mayhem when it jumped out and hopped across the school dinner hall.

"Angela, did you say that you made a phone call to me a few moments ago?"

"I cannot deny that it was me," she said, putting on a baby voice.

"But how did you know about the concrete being thrown at the car? It only happened a few hours ago."

"Kate. I was talking to her on the phone earlier this evening and she told me all about it. When she mentioned about the hanging man trick, I couldn't resist joining in the fun. Just like old times, eh?" she said, laughing.

Mike was annoyed. "So it was you who was talking to Kate. You mean to say the whole thing was just a practical joke?"

"Well, I was going to phone you anyway."

"At one o'clock in the morning?"

"That's not late is it? I really wanted you to do me a big favour. My dad has bought me a car for my birthday but he refuses to take me out driving. Says he doesn't trust me."

"I wonder why?" said Mike, sarcastically.

"I've booked a lesson with a driving school, but as we're not on the bus route, I don't know how I'm going to get there. Would you drive me into town in my car, and wait for me while I have my lesson, then bring me back home? You're my only hope. What do you say?"

"Not likely," he thought to himself. "But then, she is my cousin."

There was a pause. "Come on Mike - be a sport. I'm sorry about that stupid stunt. My dad will drive me round to your place. You don't have to pick me up here."

"Alright," he said, reluctantly.

"That's brilliant. See you tomorrow at half past two."

He put the phone down and looked out of the window. A taxi was just pulling up outside. "Oh no. It's mum and dad. I'd better make myself scarce. I'm not in the mood to explain to dad why there's going to be a huge dent in his bank balance."

"Had any weird phone calls lately?" said Kate, as Mike came into the kitchen for breakfast. Mike said nothing. He shook some cereal into a bowl, then went over to the fridge for milk. On the way back to the table, he stopped behind Kate. She stood up suddenly when she realised that he was poised to pour the contents of the bowl over her head.

"You wouldn't dare!" she shouted out, thinking that he probably would.

Mike sat down with a wicked grin on his face. "I wouldn't be too sure about that," he said mischievously. "We can all play tricks."

She sat down again, keeping her eyes fixed on Mike.

"You just wait until dad hears about…" She was cut off mid-sentence.

"About what?" said Mr Campbell, as he came into the room.

Kate smirked as she saw Mike wriggling in discomfort.

Mr Campbell sat down at the table, poured himself a glass of milk, and looked over towards Mike, suspiciously.

"Dad," said Mike, deciding to come straight to the point. "I had a bit of an accident in the car last night. There's a big dent in the bonnet and the windscreen's cracked."

"What!" shouted his dad, standing up so quickly that he knocked the glass of milk over.

Mike watched with a feeling of satisfaction as he saw the milk splash across the table and drip into Kate's lap before she could move.

"Dad! That's my new skirt you've ruined. And I was just going out to meet up with my friends, too!" She rushed off to the bathroom.

☠

Mike explained the circumstances of the accident, but it didn't make any difference to his father's temper. "I don't care if it was some local nutter. It will cost me a fortune to get it repaired. That's the last time I lend you my car," he said angrily, as he went to the garage to assess the damage.

Peace returned to the kitchen and Mike gave a sigh, relieved now that his father knew.

"I need someone to talk to." He picked up the phone and dialled. "Steve. It's Mike."

"Hi, Mike. I was going to phone you. How did the crucial date go last night? Went with a bang, I bet."

"You could say that. I completely blew it. It was a total disaster from start to finish. We couldn't get into the concert, some idiot threw a rock at the car and, to top it all, Rachael was really annoyed with me. I think she blamed me for the whole thing."

"No, - she'll just be playing hard to get. Probably loved every minute of it. When are you going to see her again?" Steve questioned.

"From the way things went, I don't think she'll want to see me again. Ever!" said Mike, despondently. "Still, why should I bother? There are plenty of other nice girls around. Nicer even than Rachael. I don't care if I never set eyes on Rachael Astley again. She can go and take a jump."

He knew he was lying because he actually felt quite upset about Rachael's parting remarks, but it seemed to be the right thing to say in front of his friend. He didn't want to make out that he cared that much.

"Good for you," said Steve, who seemed to be enjoying the drama of the situation. "Plenty more peas in the pod. Plenty more cans on the shelf. Plenty more…"

"Alright, Steve – I think I've got the message," interrupted Mike. "I was going to ask you if…"

Mike stopped talking. He'd heard a noise outside the room. "Who's that? Is it you, Kate?" The door opened and in walked Rachael. Mike raised his eyebrows in surprise. She was the last person he had expected to see that morning.

"It's your friend again. You were busy on the phone to that other girlfriend of yours, so I thought I'd let her in," said Kate spitefully, seeking to take revenge for what had happened in the kitchen.

"I'll call you back, Steve," said Mike putting down the phone. How much had Rachael heard?

Chapter 5
ZILLA

"Rachael!" Mike blurted out "What are you doing here?" It was obviously the wrong thing to say, but he had been so embarrassed by her sudden appearance that he hadn't had time to think. "How much did she hear?" Mike thought to himself.

There was an embarrassed silence as Rachael stood there.

"Uh, please - won't you sit down?" he said, moving some magazines off the settee. He tried to think of something else to say but his mind was blank.

Rachael sat down, nervously fingering a brooch that she was wearing on her coat. There was a look in her eye but Mike couldn't make out if it was annoyance, anger or sadness, or maybe it was a bit of all three.

"Your sister said you were talking to another girlfriend on the phone as I came in. Is that true?" she asked, glancing up at him.

"No it isn't!" said Mike, thinking how he was going to pay his sister back for her little remark. "She said that deliberately because we had an argument this morning. She was just trying to get at me. I was talking to my friend, Steve. Honestly, I was," he said, trying unsuccessfully to sound as if he was telling the truth. His face turned red and he looked away from Rachael, hoping that she wouldn't notice and take it as a sign of his guilt.

"Why has she come?" he thought to himself. "Should I apologise again for last night?" He took a deep breath. "Rachael, I..."

There was a loud ring on the doorbell. He was relieved. At least it would give him a moment to think. "I'll just answer that. I'll be back in a moment."

"No need to," said Kate, as she pushed the door open. "Another visitor. You *are* popular today."

She stepped to one side and let the newcomer in. Mike recognised her straight away; it was Zilla Bond, a girl from his year group. He knew that she was friendly with Rachael, as they sat together in class at school. Zilla often made a point of talking to him between lessons. Sometimes she would come and sit next to him during the lunch-break. She always seemed to be hanging round, trying to catch his attention.

He looked at her with a discerning eye as she walked in. There was something about her that he found slightly puzzling. She looked rather plain and yet he noticed that, when she made the effort to dress nicely, she could be very attractive. He watched her carefully as she walked into the room.

She didn't have many friends in school and had a reputation for being a bit aloof. He couldn't put his finger on it but something about her behaviour and appearance didn't quite add up.

Maybe it was the nervous cough that she had when she spoke. It usually sounded as if she was clearing her throat. Or perhaps it was the unusual combinations of colours that she chose to wear. You wouldn't describe her as crumpled but she wasn't sparkling, either. Her brown hair was tied back but it seemed to lack life and lay flat against her head. Her face was quite pretty but her nose seemed to dominate her other features. All of these factors, Mike quickly concluded, made her an intriguing person to know.

"Hi Mike," she said, walking over to him, smiling. She gave a slight cough. "I've just come to see Rachael. There's something that I need to tell her."

She didn't even glance at Rachael but carried on talking, looking directly into his eyes. "I haven't seen you round school much recently - have you been keeping out of my way?"

She was standing quite close to him. It was then that he remembered that that was one of the things that made him a bit wary of her. When she was speaking, she always stood a little closer than was normal, almost touching. It was a bit too close for comfort. He stepped back slightly, hoping that she wouldn't notice, and glanced over towards Rachael. She wasn't even looking, she seemed to be preoccupied with her own thoughts.

When Zilla saw him glance away, she turned towards Rachael. "I've got a message for you." She looked back at Mike then went over to the settee and sat beside her friend. Leaning over, she cupped her hand to Rachael's ear and whispered something that Mike couldn't hear. The two girls giggled for a moment then Rachael stood up.

"I'll have to go Mike, something has cropped up. I'll see you around." She turned and walked to the door, followed by Zilla. Zilla stopped just before she went out.

"See you soon," she smiled, with a lingering glance that held his eyes for a moment too long.

He watched from the window as they both walked away from the house.

"What was all that about?" he said to himself, as he sat down and switched on the television. He picked up the remote and flicked from station to station but he couldn't concentrate. He was puzzled. Why had Rachael come in the first place? Why was Zilla being so friendly and what was the message that sent them both off so quickly?

The ringing phone penetrated through his thoughts. "I bet that's Steve," he said, reaching over to pick up the phone.

"Hi. Mike speaking."

There was no reply. "Hello. Is there anyone there?"

"Yes," replied a voice that seemed to be

speaking through cotton wool. There was silence again.

"Who is this? What do you want?" said Mike, becoming concerned about the strange call.

Mike waited for a reply, not sure what to say or do. The bizarre-sounding voice cut back in again.

"I was on the bridge last night when you were passing. I dropped you a little present. Do you remember? Pity it missed, but I won't miss next time." There was a click and the line went dead.

Mike's blood froze and the colour drained away from his face, as he thought of the concrete slab smashing into the car, bouncing off the bonnet then coming through the windscreen straight at him.

Chapter 6
DEADLY PHONE CALL

Kate walked in through the door which led from the garage into the kitchen and sat down at the table. She looked over towards Mike who appeared to be slumped against the wall. His face looked grey and haggard.

"Had any good phone calls recently?" she remarked, in a casual voice.

"What do you mean?" he said, looking startled. "Were you listening in on that phone call I just had?"

It was then that he saw she was carrying their father's mobile phone in her hand.

"Where did you get that from?"

"Oh, from dad's car in the garage," she replied, trying to sound unconcerned.

Mike suddenly realised what she was hinting at. "It was you, wasn't it? You phoned me from the garage on dad's mobile phone! Just you wait!"

Kate quickly jumped up from the seat and ran round to the other side of the table, out of her brother's reach.

"That was a really sick joke, Kate. How could you do it?" he shouted, as he tried to grab her across the table.

She moved backwards, but he quickly moved round to the side, hoping to catch hold of her. Just at that moment, Mrs Campbell came in.

"Are you two at it again? I wish you'd both

grow up instead of behaving like babies."

Mike explained the situation and soon had his mum on his side.

"Kate! What happened to Mike last night was very serious. He could have been killed. It's not something to joke about."

"Alright, I'm sorry. I suppose it was a bit stupid, but you did ask for it," she said.

"Kate!" said Mrs Campbell, in a threatening voice.

"Alright. I get the message. I promise I won't do it again."

Mike seemed to be satisfied. It was the first time that he had got his sister to promise anything, but would she keep to it?

Later in the afternoon Mike sat down to do his maths homework but he was finding it very hard to concentrate.

"Why did she call round this morning? What was she going to tell me?" he mused. "Maybe she was coming round to make things up with me."

Through the window he could see the postman walking down the garden path.

"I'll try again later," he said, as he went to pick up the mail.

There was only one letter on the floor and, as he stooped to pick it up, he saw it was addressed to him.

"Who can this be from?" He pushed his finger into the corner of the envelope to open it. "I hope it's not another ticket to the next Zombies concert." He pulled out a photograph from the envelope and analysed it closely.

It was of himself, travelling in the B.M.W. as it passed under the bridge where the accident had happened. The photo showed a rock crashing through the windscreen and hitting the driver. There were red flecks of blood spraying out from his head.

"This is peculiar," he said, astonished at what he was looking at. "How can there be a photograph of an event that didn't happen?"

He looked again and found that the picture had been constructed by cutting out sections of different photos and sticking them together.

"Whoever did this must have had several photos. One of the bridge, one of my dad's car and one of me." The images had been skilfully cut out and reassembled into a single picture. The blood on the photo had been drawn on with a felt-tip pen. In the assembled photograph, he was the only one in the car. There was no picture of Rachael.

"Whoever did this must really hate me." He turned the card over and, on the back, printed in large capital letters, was the word 'DIE'.

Chapter 7
ANGELA

Enraged, he stood up holding the card in his hand.

"Why should anyone want to do this to me? Why do they hate me so much?" He paused for a moment. "Unless it was Kate. But she promised that she wouldn't play any of her silly tricks any more."

"Kate! Where are you?" he shouted.

"I'm in here!" came the reply. "What do you want?"

He walked quickly into the kitchen. Kate looked up from the magazine she was reading, as the door banged against the wall.

"Are you alright?" she said, seeing her brother's white face. He seemed to be trembling as he stood before her.

"You and your stupid tricks!" he shouted. "I'm tired of you playing your sick jokes on me! When are you going to grow up?"

"I haven't got a clue what you're talking about," she said, trying to remain calm, instead of following her natural inclination to hit back.

"Of course you know what I'm talking about!" he yelled, throwing the photograph on the table in front of her.

"I've never seen this before. It's not my style. It certainly is cleverly done though," she said, turning it over in her hands. "I promised you I wouldn't play any more games and I haven't. I didn't do this. I don't think I'd be able to do it if I tried."

"Oh, yes you did!" Mike raged. He picked up the magazine she was reading, bent it in half and threw it across the room. "Who else has got photos of me and the car?"

"Stop blaming me. I didn't do it. It wasn't me!" She put her hands to her face and burst into tears.

Mike was surprised. It was the first time he had seen his sister cry since she was a little girl.

"If I've ever played a joke on you in the past, I've always told you straight away. I've never carried it on, have I? I'm telling you, it wasn't me."

Mike reflected. What she said was true. She had always been quite open about what she had done and had never pretended otherwise. His anger began to drain away as he realised that maybe he had made a mistake.

"I'm sorry," he mumbled. "Since that incident on the bridge, I've been very edgy. It's really beginning to get to me."

"I'm sorry, too," she added. "I suppose it's partly my fault for winding you up. But, when I promised I wouldn't play any more tricks on you, I meant it."

There was a toot of a car horn outside the house. Mike looked at his watch.

"That must be Angela. I'd forgotten that I'd arranged to give her a lift into town for her driving lesson at two o'clock."

He picked his coat up and turned to go. "See you later," he said, smiling. "I'm sorry about the magazine. I'll pick a couple of new ones up when I'm in town."

As he reached the car, Angela's father was just getting out of the driver's side door.

"Would you like a lift back home?" Mike asked, as he climbed into the warm driver's seat.

"He's arranged for a taxi," Angela said.

Angela's dad leaned over to Mike, who was fastening up his seat belt.

"Pity the poor driving instructor," he said, nodding his head towards Angela and winking his eye.

"Have you thought about giving her lessons yourself?" Mike asked, politely.

"You must be joking," he grinned as looked towards his daughter. "I'd rather take a ride on a runaway bus."

"Hurry up and let's get going!" shouted Angela impatiently. "Or it will be two years before I pass my test."

Mike made himself comfortable and turned on the engine. He then reached into his pocket and pulled out the photograph.

"Before we go, do you know anything about this?" he asked gently, not wishing to make the same mistake twice.

"Urgh! Is that you with all the blood coming out of your head? Hey, wait a minute! You think I'd do something like that, do you? I'm not a sicko, Mike. Come on - stop wasting my time. Let's move it."

"Alright," said Mike, convinced that she was telling the truth. "Do you want me to explain the gears?"

"Do me a favour! I'm not a total idiot."

There was a crunch as Mike pressed the clutch and moved the floppy gear stick. "Now, the first thing you do is make sure nothing is coming before you pull out."

"Stop it!" she said indignantly. "I'm paying for a lesson from a professional. I don't want instructions from a novice. Get moving, my lesson is at two o'clock!"

Mike put the car into first gear, or so he thought. He pressed the accelerator and his neck jerked in the wrong direction as the car went into reverse. There was a faint tinkle of glass as the car bumper depressed the headlamp of the car behind.

"Thank heaven it's not my dad's B.M.W.," Mike thought as he turned around. "Let's get out of here before someone sees what we've done."

"Excuse me. Not 'we'. It's what you've done. Are you sure you passed your driving test?" quipped Angela sarcastically.

"What kind of banger is this anyway? The gears are all in the wrong place," Mike said, hitting back to hide his embarrassing mistake.

He pulled out from the kerb and proceeded

down the road feeling nervous, now he realised that Angela was watching out for any mistakes.

"What was my father saying about preferring to take a ride on a runaway bus? Looking at your driving, I think I understand how he feels," Angela scoffed.

"Why did I volunteer for this?" muttered Mike to himself. He checked the rear view mirror for the third time in ten seconds. He felt as if he was taking the driving lessons, and his cousin was the driving instructor.

He remembered back to when he was younger and Angela and Kate had combined forces against him. He had been no match for them then, and it appeared that nothing had changed.

"I'm sorry for being so snipey," she half apologised. "But that's just me."

"Don't I know it," he thought, keeping his eyes on the road.

"Take a left turn here and you can drop me at the driving school. I'll be finished in an hours' time."

Mike decided to stroll around town while he was waiting, and pick up the magazines he had promised his sister. An hour later, he returned to collect Angela at the school.

Angela moved over into the passenger seat as Mike climbed into the driver's side. He set off slowly through the busy town traffic. Eventually, they approached the first set of traffic lights at the main junction in the town centre.

"Watch out for the lights. They're changing," Angela warned.

Funny what a little knowledge can do, Mike thought to himself, as he pretended he hadn't seen them. He continued forwards, despite the fact the lights were now on amber.

"Stop. STOP!" shouted Angela, as she grabbed the dashboard and pressed an imaginary brake hard into the floor. Mike pressed the real brake and the car squealed to a halt just by the white line.

"Relax," said Mike, enjoying getting his own back. "I'm just testing your reactions," he said, looking down at her foot which was still flat against the car mat. "I think you should be able to manage the emergency stop, so long as you don't put your foot through the floor first."

Mike laughed loudly but, turning towards Angela, he could see that she wasn't amused. He glanced over her shoulder towards the fast food restaurant that was opposite the traffic lights. Suddenly he saw something that made his stomach go tight. His eyes widened with surprise as he saw Rachael sitting at one of the tables in the restaurant.

"That's Rachael," he said aloud. There was someone with her, but as she was sitting away from the window, he couldn't quite make out who it was. For a moment he thought it was

her friend Zilla, but then he realised that .
was sitting with a boy.

"I don't believe it," he muttered, as he
opened the car door and walked round to the
pavement to get a better view. He could see
quite clearly who she was sitting next to. "Rob
Murray," he whispered under his breath. "Rob
Murray, of all people."

Rob Murray was in the same class as Mike at
school, and had a reputation for being a bit of
a show off. He was well built, good looking and
a keen sportsman, and these were just some of
the reasons why Mike didn't like him.

Rachael looked up in his direction, but he
wasn't sure if she had seen him or not, and he
didn't have time to find out.

"Get back in the car, cloth head! The lights
are changing!" Angela shouted.

Mike took one last glance, then hurried
back. His heart was sinking fast as he jerked
the car away from the lights. Angela
continued talking but he didn't hear a word
she was saying.

"Rob Murray," he repeated, clenching his
fists tightly round the steering wheel. "How
could she do this to me?" He gazed blankly
in front, seeing his future swirling down a
plug hole.

Chapter 8
JEALOUSY

It was Monday morning and break time at school. Mike had been restless all weekend, thinking about Rachael and Rob Murray. He wanted to know why they had been together. He waited at the intersection of the two main corridors where he knew all the students had to pass. Eventually he caught sight of Rachael. She was walking with Zilla.

"Hello, Rachael," he said, stepping out in front of them. "Can we talk for a moment?"

"Hi Mike," Zilla cheerfully butted in. "I've been hearing things about you." She turned towards Rachael. "I'll see you later."

"Can we sit down for a minute?" he said, gesturing towards a nearby bench.

"If you like," she replied rather coldly. She moved over towards the seat.

Mike came straight to the point. "I saw you on Saturday sitting with Rob Murray in McDonalds. Why were you out with him?"

"I don't have to answer to you about what I do in my spare time," she replied sharply, "but while we're on the subject, I saw you driving through town with another girl. If you think you're going to play around at my expense then you can think again!"

"That was my cousin, Angela. I was giving her a lift into town so that she could take a driving lesson."

"What a likely story! I don't want to see you again and I don't want you prying into my business!" She stood up without even looking at him and walked off down the corridor.

For the rest of the morning, Mike felt confused and bitter, and found it difficult to concentrate on his work. He was annoyed that he seemed to have driven Rachael further away and he was very angry with Rob Murray. "If it wasn't for him, none of this would have happened. He has come butting in between me and Rachael – I was the one who asked her out. Why couldn't he keep his nose out?"

He stopped and paused for a moment. "Was it Rob who dropped the concrete from the bridge and sent me the photograph? It's got to be somebody who knows me, and Rob has a motive. He's jealous of me and Rachael. Steve probably told him that I was seeing her and he doesn't like the competition. It must be him."

By midday he was steaming. He hadn't completed his maths work and, as a result, he had to go back into class during his lunch-break to finish off. After he had eaten his sandwiches, he made his way to the cloakroom to pick up a pen from his jacket. As soon as he walked in, he noticed Rob Murray there, putting something away in his bag. Mike looked around and checked that they were alone.

Knowing that there wasn't enough room for two people to pass side by side between the coat pegs, Mike came up to Rob and deliberately elbowed him to one side.

"Hey! Watch where you're going," Rob Murray said, annoyed at being pushed by Mike.

"Why should I?" said Mike, seeing this as an opportunity to get even with his rival.

Mike stood in front of him and pushed him back towards the coat hooks, blocking his escape.

"I saw you with Rachael at the weekend. Did you ask her out?"

"That's none of your business!" said Rob, trying to edge past Mike.

"Oh, yes it is! I've already asked her out. We've got something going."

Without any warning, Rob, realising that he was cornered, gave a quick blow to Mike's chest which sent him sprawling on the floor.

Mike stood up with fists raised, ready to fight. This was just the opportunity that he had been waiting for.

Chapter 9
THE FIGHT

Mike launched himself forwards with his fists flying. He was the taller and heavier of the two and had every reason to be confident of winning. He swung a punch, but Rob ducked and his clenched fist smashed into the steel coat hangers. Before he had time to feel the pain, Rob grabbed him round the neck and wrestled him to the ground. They found themselves tangled in the coats and anoraks as they struggled to their feet, each one trying to gain the advantage.

With tremendous effort, Mike managed to release his head from Rob's firm grip. They separated and stood back for a moment, facing each other again. It was not going to be quite as easy as Mike expected. Rob was stronger and faster than he had imagined. They circled round each other like two wild animals, watching for any sign of weakness. Mike was ready to begin another attack.

"What on earth are you doing?" asked a voice, coming from the side. Mike, thinking it might be one of the teachers, was startled and turned to look.

Rob immediately saw his advantage and, closing his fist tightly, landed a punch squarely on Mike's nose. Mike reeled backwards and his vision went blurred. He felt himself falling to the ground, banging his head quite hard on a nearby metal radiator.

He tried to get to his feet, but soon realised he couldn't keep his balance. Slumping back to the ground, he felt his head spinning and his nose was hurting quite badly. He sat there, looking upwards at Rob who was waiting, ready, in case he got to his feet.

Mike knew he was defeated. He felt the blood trickling down his nose and onto his white shirt. He put his hand on his head and felt a bump the size of a small egg.

He was beaten but his spirit wasn't broken.

"You wait!" he said, pointing towards Rob. "I'll get you back for this! I know you're the one who threw the concrete at me from the bridge, and you also sent that photograph, just because you were jealous of me and Rachael."

"I don't know what you're talking about," replied Rob, with a sneer. "You'd better not try it on with me again, or I'll give you something else to think about."

"You were lucky!" shouted Mike, as Rob walked away.

"Are you alright Mike?"

He turned round to see who was speaking.

"Zilla - it's you. I thought you were one of the teachers. When I turned round, he planted me one, right on the nose."

"You poor thing. Here, let me help you," she said, taking a tissue from her pocket. She gently wiped the blood away from his nose and tried to clean his shirt.

"How does that feel?" she asked, gently stroking his head.

He touched his nose. "Ow! It's sore, but I don't think it's broken."

"You've got a huge bump on your head," she said, as she continued to run her hands gently through his hair. "There, I'll kiss it better."

Mike laughed. "You sound like my mum. She used to say that to me when I was younger."

"What were you fighting about, Mike?"

"Nothing. It doesn't matter."

She put her arms around his shoulders. "Come on, I'll help you to your feet," she said. As he stood up, she pulled him towards her as if to embrace him. "Are you sure you're okay?"

"I feel a bit groggy, but I'll be alright soon."

"Let's go to the coffee bar and I'll buy you a drink," she said, linking his arm and leading him down the corridor.

Mike felt a bit unsteady and was quite glad that someone was helping him, even if it was Zilla. He sat down and waited while she went over to the counter and ordered their drinks.

"Here sip this," she said, as she pushed a

strong, black cup of coffee across the table and sat down next to him.

Just then, Rachael strolled into the coffee bar. She turned her head when she heard familiar voices and was astonished by what she saw.

"So this is how you spend your lunch-break? And you've got the cheek to ask me about being with Rob Murray!" She ran off, back down the corridor.

"Rachael, I was only...!" Mike shouted after her, but it was too late, she had disappeared out of sight.

Zilla just grinned and didn't seem to be the slightest bit bothered. "Don't worry, she'll get over it."

Mike pulled himself away. "I've got to get going. I'm due in class."

When school was finished, Mike wanted to get home as quickly as possible. He wasn't feeling all that brilliant and he didn't want to talk to anyone. He went over to his locker to put away some books. As he unlocked the door, he noticed a strange, putrid smell - as if something inside was rotting. It was then that he saw dark, red liquid dripping from underneath his locker door. Standing back in horror, he watched as a small river of crimson gore slowly dripped down over the metallic surface onto the floor.

Chapter 10
HALLOWE'EN PARTY

"What's this?" he cried, running his finger along the bottom edge of the door. Surely it couldn't be blood? It must be red ink or tomato ketchup. He couldn't tell.

He carefully opened his locker. To his horror, he found a gory mass of chicken giblets and entrails, all strewn about. His books and P.E. kit were swimming in blood and slimy tissue.

"Urgh! I don't believe this! Who is doing this to me!" he yelled. "Why me?"

He went over to the waste bin close by and pulled out the black bin-liner. He took his books out of the locker and shook them until the thick clots of blood slid off. Next, he rolled up his sleeves, cupped his hands and slopped the repulsive entrails into the bag. He felt as if he was going to be sick as they fell into the black plastic bag. It was then that he noticed a piece of paper which was attached to the back of his locker. He held it in his blood-stained hands and read the printed message: 'This is how you will look when I've finished with you.'

Mike shook his head in disbelief. "Someone around here is really very sick."

"Mike, I've been looking for you," said a voice from behind him, but he wasn't listening. The message had shaken him and he was finding it hard to focus.

"Mike! Are you alright?" repeated the voice.

"Oh, not Zilla again," thought Mike, as he registered the fact that someone was speaking to him.

He turned round. "Oh, it's you, Kate. I thought it was Zilla."

"Mike!" shouted Kate urgently, when she saw that her brother's hands were covered in blood. "Have you cut yourself?"

She examined him carefully and saw that his face was also covered in bruises. "What's going on? What's happened to your hands and face? You look awful!"

"I found this in my locker," he said, opening the bin-liner and showing her the contents.

"Yuck," she said, as the smell reached her nose. "How could anyone do such a thing?"

"There's more," he said, showing her the threatening message. It was obvious from her response that she had nothing to do with it.

She took him to a nearby sink where he washed his hands and cleaned himself up.

"This is getting pretty serious," she said as they walked down the corridor. "Do you think we should call the police?"

"No. I've got a pretty good idea who did this and I'm going to handle it my own way. Don't worry about me, I can give as good as I get."

54

Mike stopped. "Listen, Kate. Thanks for your help, but I'm feeling much better. I'll see you at home later on." He turned around and walked off in the opposite direction.

It was Friday evening and Mike had arranged to meet Steve at his house. He stood in front of the mirror examining his recently rearranged features. The swelling on his nose and head had gone down and he almost felt normal again.

"Thank goodness there's no permanent damage," he thought, as he ran his finger along the line of his nose. He had taken a couple of days off school, not because he didn't feel well, but because he didn't want Rachael to see him looking like a fighter who had just lost a boxing match.

"Who is it tonight, handsome? Is it Rachael again?" said Kate, as she caught sight of him preening himself in the mirror.

"I wish it was," he replied. "I'm only going to Steve's house. I'll see you later on."

It was ten minutes walk to Steve's house and, on the way, Mike called into the local garage shop to pick up a video and a couple of cans of coke.

"Fancy spending the evening with Steve when I should be out with Rachael," he muttered to himself, as he knocked on his friend's door. "But what can I do about it? Rob Murray won't have wasted any time once he finds that Rachael has fallen out with me."

Steve opened the door. "Let's see what you've chosen," he said. "*The Midnight Murderer*. Seen it. That's the one where he cuts people's heads off with a chain saw, isn't it?"

"Well, you're going to see it again," said Mike, pushing the video into his hand. He wasn't going to go back to the shop and change it.

Steve put the tape into the player and they both settled down to watch the film.

"This is the exciting part," Steve said, sitting on the edge of his seat with his eyes fixed on the screen.

The bell in the church tower was chiming twelve and the sound of a growling chain saw was echoing through the graveyard.

Mike yanked the ring pull on his can and put the can to his lips.

"Steve," Mike ventured, between gulps.

"Just watch this bit."

"Steve. What do you think of me and Rachael? Have I got a chance with her?"

"This is where he jumps out from the dark passage with the chain saw."

Mike leaned forwards and switched off the set.

"Hey! What are you doing? That's one of the best bits of the film!"

"Forget about the video for a minute, Steve, can't you? What about me and Rachael? The last time I saw her, she said she didn't want to see me again. I think she likes Rob Murray, but what am I going to do about it?"

"Forget about her. Let's have a night out at the bowling alley with the rest of the guys, like we used to," suggested Steve.

"I wish I could forget, but I can't, and it's driving me mad. If I find out she's seeing Rob Murray..."

"Let's go to a club in town. You might meet someone else."

"I'm not interested in anybody else."

Steve was silent for a moment. He realised that Mike wasn't in the mood to be distracted.

"Have you heard about the Hallowe'en party that's on tomorrow night?"

"No, I've been off school for the last two days. It sounds interesting - tell me more."

"It's being held in the old derelict mansion that's just off the main road as you leave town. About ten of us from school are going down tomorrow afternoon to clean the place up for the party. We're bringing some food and making decorations. Everyone in the school year group is invited, but you have to come in fancy dress."

Mike looked enthusiastic. "I could ask Rachael."

Steve pulled his face. "Why are you so struck on her? She's nothing special."

"Steve, I've got to go," said Mike, standing up. Now the idea had been planted in his head, he knew he couldn't rest until he'd phoned Rachael.

"But what about the video? It's only halfway through. There's another five heads to be chopped off yet."

"Thanks, Steve, but I think I've seen it before. I'll see you at the party tomorrow evening."

Mike walked home at a brisk pace. The party had given him a reason to contact Rachael again. Surely she wouldn't say no if he invited her? As soon as he arrived home, he picked up the phone and began to dial her number.

"Could I speak to Rachael, please?" he asked, as her mother answered the phone.

"It's your young man," he heard her calling to Rachael.

"Which one?" he heard Rachael reply. His heart sank.

"What does she mean 'which one'?" he thought to himself.

"It's me, Rachael," he said.

"Who's me?"

"It's Mike. Don't you recognise my voice?"

"Oh, you," she said, sounding disappointed.

"Were you expecting someone else?" asked

Mike, surprised by the slightly unenthusiastic response. "Rachael, there's a Hallowe'en party at the old house just outside town, tomorrow evening. Would you like to go with me?"

There was a long pause on the other end of the phone.

"Yes, that sounds interesting," Rachael replied, finally.

"I'll pick you up at eight o'clock tomorrow evening and, don't forget, you need to come in fancy dress. See you then."

Mike put the phone down slowly. "Yessssssss!" he cried out, and did a little dance around the room to celebrate. "Roll on tomorrow! I can't wait!"

It was the next morning before Mike thought about the transport problem. It wasn't quite the same taking someone out on the bus as it was in a car. He looked over towards his father who was reading the paper at the table, and wondered if there was any chance of getting the car again after last time.

"He can only say no," Mike thought to himself.

"Dad."

"No," answered his father, looking up from his paper. "There is no possibility whatsoever of you borrowing the car, so don't even ask."

"He must be a mind-reader," Mike concluded,

as he hadn't even managed to ask the question.

"But I will give you a lift there and back. Kate is going and she has already asked me."

Just at that moment, Kate walked into the room.

"You're not going to the Hallowe'en party. It isn't for your year group," said Mike, sternly.

"I've been invited by that cute boy, Nigel Smith, and I'm taking Angela along as well," said Kate with a grin.

"Nigel Smith! He's about as cute as the back of a bus," said Mike, disdainfully. "Some party it's going to be with my sister and cousin keeping an eye on everything I do," he moaned to himself.

☠

By seven-thirty, Mike was putting the finishing touches to his Dracula costume. He had plastered his hair back with gel, and had a pair of false fangs in his mouth, which made it rather hard to talk. Kate had powdered his face white and had put some of their mum's bright red lipstick on his lips, and dark liner on his eyebrows. He was dressed all in black with a cloak over his shoulders.

Kate and Angela were dressed as witches and were waiting in the car, ready to go.

"Come on dad," said Mike impatiently. His dad was watching a football match on the TV. "It's time to go and the hags in the back of the

60

car are getting restless."

Ten minutes later they pulled up outside Rachael's house. "Oh no! Not another one," said Kate giggling, as she saw that Rachael was also dressed as a witch.

Mike jumped out of the car. "I'll carry your broomstick, Rachael!" he called out as he opened the door for her. "There's room for one more in the back. Great costume you're wearing," he said, as he held her pointed hat while she climbed into the car.

"Flattery will get you everywhere," she responded cheerfully.

"You never said our costumes were great and we're all dressed the same," Angela complained.

"Either you've got it or you haven't and I'm afraid you two don't have it... - ouch!" he shouted out as a broomstick clipped the back of his head.

By the time Mr Campbell dropped them off at the old house it was dark.

"I'll pick you all up at half past eleven," he shouted through the window as he drove away.

The house was a short distance off the main road and there was only the occasional car headlight to illuminate the path.

"I'll just hold your hand, Rachael, so that you don't fall into the ditch," Mike whispered.

Rachael just smiled.

"There are no lights on in the house," said Kate, as they approached the front door. "Are you sure we're at the right place?"

"It must be," insisted Mike. "There's no other old house in the area. Perhaps the people who were setting the place up have gone home to get changed and haven't come back yet. Let's go inside and see."

Mike led the way as the three witches followed. He pushed open the front door and felt along the wall for the light switch, but he couldn't find it.

He remembered he'd picked up his dad's lighter on the way out of the house, in case they had to light candles at the party. The flame leapt up as he flicked the top. The small, bright light illuminated the room and they all walked in, huddled together in a tight bunch. There was a scuttling noise in the corner and Angela screamed as she saw a large rat scramble across the floor.

"I hate rats!" she shouted. "Come on - there's no one here. Let's get out and phone up your dad to take us home. We must have come to the wrong place."

There was another scraping noise and Rachael cried out, as she saw a spider as big as a fist dart across the room. Even Mike, who wasn't particularly bothered by rats, had a very strong dislike of spiders the size of a tennis ball.

"I think you're right," he said, giving into his natural squeamishness. "We must have made a mistake. Let's get out of here!"

As they turned to go, he felt something slimy and slithery land on his neck. He reacted instinctively, ducking quickly and brushing the back of his head violently, as if he was being attacked by a nest of wasps. The lighter in his hand dropped to the floor and went out.

"What's wrong, Mike?" shouted Rachael, who couldn't see what was happening, but could hear him thrashing around. "There's something on the back of my neck!" he said fearfully, as he lashed out wildly in all directions.

Whatever it was, it dropped off and onto the feet of Angela, who let out a terrified cry.

"It's on the floor! I just felt it wriggle over my foot!"

There was total confusion as Mike and the three girls struggled to find their way back out of the room, in darkness.

Suddenly they all stopped. Something or someone had switched on a bright torch. They all held up their hands in front of their eyes to block the dazzle, and stood like rabbits caught in the blaze of a car headlamp, unable to move, motionless with fear. A low moaning noise started, which at first seemed to come from the direction of the window, but gradually swelled to fill the whole room.

The lights came on and they were astounded to see that the room was filled with ghosts and monsters, all moaning in unison.

"Happy Hallowe'en party!" someone

shouted out, and the gathered ghouls broke out into fits of laughter.

"Oh, very funny," said Mike, sitting down in the nearest chair to recover his composure.

"You've got to admit, it was a good joke," sniggered Steve, as he pulled a rubber rat and spider across the floor on a piece of string.

Nigel Smith was standing on a balcony, holding a rubber snake tied to a long piece of elastic, which he was lowering down upon their heads.

Kate didn't look very pleased.

"About as cute as the back of a bus," Mike growled through his teeth.

"Come on, it was only a bit of fun. You were the last ones here so we decided to play a few tricks. Lighten up and chill out."

Mike looked around the room. It was obvious that a lot of time had been spent getting the place into some kind of shape for the party. There was a large poster saying "Hallowe'en Rave," spread across one of the walls, and at the far side of the room there was a table with food and drink. A large net full of coloured balloons was attached to the ceiling, waiting to be released later on in the evening.

The music started and within a few moments, everyone was on the floor dancing. Mike and the girls joined in the fun and quickly forgot their frightening entrance. After half an hour on the floor, Rachael took a break and sat down on a bench at the side of the room.

64

"I'm thirsty, Mike. Would you get me a drink of coke please?"

"Sure," said Mike. "I'll be back in a minute."

He made his way through the crowded room, over to the refreshment table.

"Great party," said Steve, as Mike picked up a sausage roll. "I'm sorry if you were scared when you came in, but it was only a laugh."

"I wasn't scared," said Mike, lying through his teeth. "I was just a bit concerned for the girls. You know what they're like with mice and rats."

Steve just laughed as Mike poured two cupfuls of coke from a large plastic bottle.

"Who's that dancing with Rachael?" Steve asked, straining his neck to see across the room.

"She's taking a break from dancing at the moment. It must be someone else," Mike said confidently, as he popped a piece of cheese into his mouth.

"Nope. It's definitely her. She's dancing with Rob Murray. You're going to have to do something about that, Mike. He's stealing your girl."

Mike made his way back as quickly as he could, over to where Rachael was dancing.

"I've brought your drink!" he shouted over the music, trying to catch her attention. He could see that Rob Murray was saying something to Rachael and she was laughing.

"He's not going to get away with this," Mike thought to himself as he pushed his way through the dancers towards Rachael, holding the two drinks. "Rachael!" he shouted again.

Rob Murray turned around to face Mike and, as he did so, bumped into the two cups of coke that he was carrying. Mike was soaked as the sticky liquid splashed over his arms and down his trousers. He let the paper cups fall to the ground and squared up to Rob Murray.

He suddenly felt a tug at his arm as someone tried to pull him out of the group of dancers, to the outside of the room.

He turned and saw it was Zilla. "What did you do that for?" he said angrily.

"Come over here," she said, drawing him over to a quiet part of the room. "I'm sorry I had to do that, but I could see what was going to happen."

"I know what was going to happen, you don't have to tell me. I was going to punch Rob Murray for dancing with Rachael!"

"Don't be stupid. It's a party, isn't it? There's no harm in Rachael dancing with someone else. Anyhow, you were about to make a fool of yourself."

"What do you mean?"

"Look what happened last time you picked a fight with Rob Murray."

"He got lucky last time."

Zilla reached over to the table and picked up a couple of paper napkins. "You're soaking," she said, and she began to dry him off. "Come and have a dance with me." She drew him back onto the floor, but well away from where Rob and Rachael were dancing. "I'm sure Rachael won't mind, and anyway, I think she's occupied at the moment."

Mike pulled himself away from Zilla. He was still smouldering over the incident. "I'm sticky and uncomfortable. I think I'll go to the bathroom and see if I can clean myself up properly."

Zilla reluctantly let go of his hand as he made his way across to the staircase. He glanced over his shoulder and scowled as he saw that Rachael was still on the floor dancing with Rob Murray.

The bathroom was up two flights of stairs on the far side of the house. The sound of the music faded slightly as he rounded the corner at the top of the second flight. The corridor leading to the bathroom was gloomy and as he made his way along, he noticed the wallpaper was peeling off the wall, and the strong, musty smell of the place made him feel slightly sick. The air seemed thick and heavy.

He reached the bathroom door and found a switch on the outside wall which he turned on. He looked through the door and could see a large room illuminated by a dull, yellow light bulb.

"I could fit my bedroom in here twice," he thought, as he went over to the sink. The washbasin was stained brown where the taps had been dripping, and there was a big crack along the bottom of the bowl. He turned on the large, brass taps, wet his face and glanced in the scratched mirror.

He spun round on his heels, startled, as he thought he'd seen a shadow flit across the open door, but in the dim light he couldn't be sure. The next moment, the light went out. It was pitch black as there were no street lights shining in from the outside.

"Alright - who's playing silly idiots?" he said out loud.

There was a noise at the door and then he heard it close with a bang, which was followed by the sound of a key turning in the lock.

"Oh no! Someone's locked me in! Wait till I get my hands on whoever's done this. Hey! Open the door!" He made his way slowly across the room, keeping his arms outstretched in front of him in the pitch blackness. Reaching the door he found it was, indeed, locked.

"That's strange," he thought, as he heard the quiet pad of footsteps coming from somewhere by the sink. Then, slowly, he began to realise what had happened. Someone had turned the light off, slipped into the room and locked the door from the inside.

He stood up straight and listened carefully.

He could hear a faint sound from the other side of the room, like someone breathing. There was a soft rustle of clothes, but his own heart was pounding away so loudly in his ears that he was uncertain.

"Who's there?" he said, trying to sound confident and unafraid. "Come on. Answer me. I know there's someone there."

There was only one way to find out. He started to make his way slowly across the room in the direction of the breathing sound. He stopped suddenly. What if it was the person who put the giblets into his locker, and threw the rock at the car?

"Is that you, Rob? Stop fooling around. This isn't a joke anymore!"

His mouth went dry and he began to sweat with fear. There could be a potential murderer in the room with him.

"HELP!" he shouted, but the sound only came out as a strangled gasp.

Chapter 11
HERE COMES DRACULA

Mike felt faint and completely disorientated, not knowing which direction he had come from or where the door was. He knelt down on one knee because he thought he would lose his balance if he didn't. Keeping completely still so that the other person wouldn't know where he was, he concentrated on how he was going to get out.

Hearing a faint rustling sound in front of him, he decided that the only choice he had was to try to grab hold of whoever it was.

"I can't see them, but at least they can't see me, either," he calculated, as he moved silently forwards. Reaching the sink, he stopped, sensing that the intruder was just a couple of feet away.

He was sure that they hadn't moved because he had been listening very carefully. He crouched down again and prepared to jump, but his knee cracked and suddenly the other person moved quickly out of reach, as if they knew what he was about to do.

Mike felt a little bolder. At least they hadn't attacked him. If they had wanted to, that would have been an ideal opportunity. Why didn't they? Perhaps the other person was afraid, also.

Hearing another faint movement, he stood up and moved in the direction the sound had come from. Something brushed across his face. He stepped back for a moment but then realised it was a piece of cord hanging from the ceiling which was used to turn the bathroom light on.

Pulling the switch, he had to shield his eyes from the sudden brightness. Facing him he saw a horrid, gnarled and twisted face. The demon-like shape turned towards the door as if it was about to run. Mike hurled himself at the fleeing figure and wrestled it to the ground. If this was the person who had been threatening him, then he was determined that he was going to get even.

The bizarre creature rolled over trying to throw Mike off, but he held on grimly, tightening his grip around its neck. He squeezed harder and harder. He wanted to inflict as much pain as possible.

"Stop! You're breaking my neck!" shouted a muffled voice. It seemed vaguely familiar but it didn't have time to register - he was about to deliver a crushing blow to the body.

"You're strangling me, Mike! It's me, Angela! Let go! I can't breath!"

"Angela!" said Mike relaxing his iron grip. "I can't believe it. Why did you do such a crazy thing? I could have really hurt you!"

"It is a Hallowe'en party," said Angela, picking herself off the floor, taking off her mask and rubbing her sore neck. "You know - party, fun, jokes, trick-or-treat? Look at the state of my hat. I spent all afternoon making it and now it's ruined."

"Serves you right," said Mike. "You scared the wits out of me. I thought I was about to be murdered."

Just at that moment, there was a grating sound at the door as if someone had pushed something into the lock from the outside. "What was that?" said Mike, walking over to have a look.

He tried to open the door. "It's still locked. Give me the key," he said to Angela.

"That's odd. I can't get the key into the lock." Bending down he peered into the keyhole and discovered the reason why.

"Someone has jammed another key into the outside of the lock, which means we can't open the door from the inside."

Angela came over to have a try but soon gave up.

"Oh, great." she said despondently. "That's a stupid trick to play. We're going to miss the party unless we can find a way out."

"That's clever coming from you. I can guess whose done it. Someone who would like to see me out of the way so that he can move in on Rachael. Well, he won't keep me in here for long. I'm getting out of this place even if it means I have to break the door down."

Angela looked up at him with admiration.

Mike stepped back, balanced himself, then ran at the door, shoulders first. The door hardly shook. He aimed a kick at one of the wooden panels, but only managed to hurt his foot. "Victorian doors," said Mike, angrily. "Even Superman would have a hard job going through that one."

"Any more bright ideas?" said Angela, sarcastically.

"We could try shouting," Mike suggested.

They both went over to the door and began shouting as loud as they could. Unfortunately, being two floors up and on the wrong side of the house, they couldn't be heard over the loud dance music from downstairs. Eventually they gave up.

Mike sat down next to Angela. "We could be here all night unless we can think of a way to get out," he said wearily.

"Thanks for being so positive," said Angela. Curling her arms round her knees, she added, "I'm cold."

Two hours later, they were still trapped in the room.

"What time is it?" asked Angela, who was, by now, feeling tired and fed up.

"Twelve o'clock."

The music downstairs had stopped. "The party must be finishing."

Angela turned to Mike. "There must be some way out of here," she said. "Have a look in your pockets, we've looked everywhere else. There might be something we could use."

Mike turned them out. There were a few coins, his set of Dracula fangs and a penknife.

"You brainless idiot!" said Angela, snatching up the penknife. "You've had this in your pocket all the time."

"So what? You can't cut your way through a door with that."

"Who mentioned cutting?" Angela opened up the penknife and began to unscrew the door lock. A moment later, the metal cover came off. She could now see the other key that had been deliberately jammed in the lock. With the penknife she managed to prise it out, leaving the lock free. She took the proper key and opened the door.

"Brilliant!" said Mike, clearly impressed by his cousin's housebreaking skills.

"Look at this," said Mike, pointing to a piece of paper that was pinned to the wall of the corridor. "OUT OF ORDER. PLEASE USE BATHROOM ON NEXT FLOOR DOWN."

"Whoever locked the door didn't want anyone to find us." They made their way downstairs where they found Steve, Zilla and a few others tidying up from the party.

"Where have you two been for the last few hours?" Steve asked, when he saw them walking down the stairs.

"Where are Rachael and Kate?" enquired Mike.

Steve turned towards him. "Your dad came to collect you at half past eleven, but, when he couldn't find you, Kate said you must have gone off somewhere together."

"Did Rachael go with them?" Mike asked anxiously.

"No. She said she was going to wait for you to come back. She didn't look very happy though, and when you didn't return, Rob Murray said he would take her back home because she didn't have a lift."

"I'll bet he did! Just wait till I see him next week. I'll give him more than a piece of my mind!"

"Anything wrong?" Steve asked.

"No, nothing at all. He's just locked us in the bathroom for the last two hours, that's all."

He turned towards Angela. "Come on. I'll walk you home."

"No need for that," said Steve. "It's a long way out of your way. Zilla lives close by Angela, so they can walk home together."

Mike looked towards Angela and she nodded. "Alright then. I'll see you around."

Mike walked out into the cold night air, angry and frustrated. It was a long walk home but at least it might help to get rid of some of the anger and bitterness he felt towards Rob Murray.

He turned to the right and walked along the main road heading towards town. "Six miles. That will take me at least two hours unless I take the short cut."

The short cut was only half the distance, but it would take him along some very dark, country lanes and across the bridge where the concrete-throwing incident had happened. Just thinking about it made him feel nervous.

He came to the junction where the road divided. It was at this point that he had to make the decision about which way he should go. He stopped and thought as he peered down the dark lane which led away from the bright lights of the town. He felt slightly uneasy about the prospect of taking this route, but it would save him an hour. He stopped and listened. Nothing stirred, not even the sound of passing traffic.

"I'll be alright," he said, loudly enough to give himself confidence. "No one is going to be around at this hour of the morning, apart from a few rabbits. And if someone is going to be frightened, it's not going to be me."

He took out his pair of luminous fangs and slipped them into his mouth. Turning off the main road, he ran down the dark lane with his cloak flying behind him in the wind. "Here comes Dracula!"

Chapter 12
RUN FOR YOUR LIFE

Down the dark road he ran until he began to feel tired. "I'm not as fit as I should be," he said to himself, as he slowed down to a walking pace. "If a car comes along, I might try to hitch a lift."

The road which appeared pitch black at first seemed to lighten up as his eyes got used to the darkness. He picked up a stick which he found lying on the grass verge, thinking that it would prevent him from falling over anything in the road. "A dead body for instance," he joked to himself, trying to keep his spirits up. Having the stick in his hand made him feel a bit more confident. At least he would have a weapon if someone did attack him.

"What am I thinking about? Why should someone attack me? It's one o'clock in the morning and there's no one about but me."

He continued down the lane trying to think about pleasant things but, all the while, the fear of crossing the bridge was growing in his mind, even though he didn't admit it to himself. "Once I'm over the bridge, I can jog for a while and I'll soon be home."

You've got to get over the bridge first, a voice spoke in his head.

"Stop thinking about it. Nothing's going to happen," he said to himself, annoyed that crossing the bridge was becoming a big issue.

Eventually, he reached the part of the lane where the road bent to the right, just before the bridge. He found himself creeping forwards, making sure that his shoes didn't make any noise as they made contact with the road. Once he was round the bend, he stopped and looked ahead. He felt a growing sense of unease. Just at that moment, the moon rose from behind a cloud and cast a faint yellow glow along the road.

He looked ahead and his heart nearly stopped. There was someone standing on the bridge. Drawing back into the shadows, he carefully looked again. The moon passed behind a cloud and he quickly realised that what he had been looking at was just the moon reflecting on the parapet of the bridge.

"You dim-wit. There's no one there. It's only a shadow cast by the moon. I've been fooled by that before."

Turn back before it's too late, a voice said inside his head.

"What? Turn round and have to walk all that extra distance? Not likely."

He stepped out of the shadows and made his way towards the bridge. He hummed a tune loudly and scuffed his shoes along the road, making as much noise as he dared to.

He arrived at the centre of the bridge and stood there looking down onto the road. It was the first time he'd been back to the spot since the night he went out with Rachael to see the concert. He leaned over the edge, looking at the road below, trying to imagine why anyone would possibly want to throw a lump of stone at a passing car.

"It's turned one o'clock and here's me, standing on a bridge in the middle of the country," he said to himself, feeling proud at having conquered his own fears.

At that moment he heard a twig crack. The sound came from back the way he had just come, and sent a shiver of fear up his spine. He looked into the darkness but couldn't see anything. "Probably a fox prowling round," he said to himself, as he quickly turned and walked the rest of the way across the bridge.

He felt a great desire to break into a run but he knew that if he did, he would finish up in a panic. Walking on as fast as he could, he frequently glanced over his shoulder to make sure nothing was following him.

He came to another bend in the road; soon the bridge would be out of sight. He stopped and turned round, confident that the worst part of the journey was behind him. As he looked back, the moon came out and illuminated the area with a faint glow.

"That parapet on the bridge always seems to look like a person when the moon shines on it," he said, thankful that it was only an illusion.

Suddenly, what he thought was the parapet, moved. His eyes widened; he couldn't believe what he was seeing. Surely it was his imagination. A shadowy figure was walking towards him.

Mike swung around and began to run down the road, turning every few moments to see if the thing following him was in sight. It was. He ran on, partly relieved that the figure behind wasn't gaining on him.

"Only another few hundred yards and I'm back on the main road which is well lit. I've just got to keep going," he gasped.

He turned once again, but this time, to his horror, he saw that the gap between himself and his pursuer was closing. He knew that if he continued, he would be caught by the maniac who was following him.

Without pausing to think, he plunged off the lane into the thick undergrowth and trees that grew at the side of the road. He pushed his way through, oblivious of the nettles and brambles that clawed at his clothes.

"What am I going to do? He'll hear me crashing through this undergrowth. He'll easily be able to follow me and catch me." Finding himself stuck in the middle of a thick rhododendron bush which he couldn't get through, he decided that the only way out was to go back a few feet and try another route.

He stopped and looked back in the direction he had just come from.

He could see the road and the gap where he had plunged through. Suddenly, a shadow appeared in the opening. It stopped and looked forwards as if it was scanning the darkness for his scent. The hairs on the back of Mike's neck stood on end. If he made a sound the shadow would know his position immediately.

The phantom pulled something from its belt. Something which glinted in the pale light of the moon.

"He's got a knife!" Mike trembled with terror. "He's going to kill me."

He thought of the blood oozing from his school locker and the threatening message. His arm started to shake. He held it tightly by his side until it stopped moving. The creature advanced into the undergrowth slowly, stopping every few paces and listening, then lifting its nose as if it was sniffing the air. It moved slowly in his direction, until it came to a stop - directly by the rhododendron bush where Mike was hiding.

Mike couldn't see the monster's face, but he could see that in his hand he carried a long, sharp, cruel-looking knife. He gripped the stick he had been carrying, very tightly. At least if he was discovered, he would have a weapon to strike back with.

Much to his relief, the figure passed on, going further into the wood. When he was far enough away, Mike crept out of the bush and made his way back to where he had left the lane. He reached the road and began to run as fast as he could.

He knew he had been seen because he heard a loud noise in the bushes. Mike ran on towards the main road, finding new strength to keep going.

He could hear his assailant closing from behind. Just at that moment, a car appeared from round the bend. Mike ran into its path, desperate to stop the car which swerved to avoid him. There was a screech of tyres as it skidded to a halt.

"You're going to get yourself killed!" he heard a voice shout.

"Could I have a lift? I've hurt myself," said Mike, hoping desperately that the man would say yes. He looked at Mike suspiciously, but when he saw his hands were scratched and bleeding, he agreed.

As the car sped off, Mike caught sight of the shadowy figure standing by the roadway.

Ten minutes later, he arrived back at his house. He thanked the driver and proceeded to open his front door. Once he was in the living room he took off his cloak and collapsed in a heap on the settee.

"I've survived," he said, as he began peeling off the rest of his Dracula costume. "That was the worst night of my life."

It's not over yet... whispered a strange voice in his head.

A moment later the phone rang. Mike gave a nervous shudder and he felt the muscles in his body tense up.

"Surely not again? Please, don't let it happen again." He pressed the record button on the stereo near the phone, then slowly picked up the receiver and placed it to his ear.

"I nearly got you tonight. It's only a matter of time before you DIE."

There was a screaming laugh and the phone went dead.

Chapter 13
HORROR IN THE NIGHT

Mike slowly made his way up the stairs. His legs were so heavy, he felt as if he was wearing lead boots. He fell onto his bed and lay there, too tired to get changed.

"What am I going to do? Should I contact the police? What about telling my parents? Kate knows, but she doesn't realise how serious things are. She still thinks it's a bit of a joke."

He looked at his watch and saw it was two o'clock. He yawned and he felt his body relaxing.

"At least I can forget all about this for a few hours," he thought, as he drifted into a deep sleep.

It was sometime later when he was woken again. Something was banging outside. He looked at the clock and saw it was ten to four.

"I've only been asleep for two hours. I'm going to be shattered in the morning." He turned over and forced his eyes closed. He was just about to fall asleep when there was another bang. He sat up in bed, annoyed that something was keeping him awake.

Listening carefully, he realised that the wind

was rising outside. The bang came again, so he decided to get out of bed to investigate. At the bottom of the garden there was a greenhouse. Its window was open, and it was this that was flapping in the wind.

"I'm never going to be able to get any sleep with that racket," he muttered to himself. He pulled on his trainers.

Mike quietly made his way down the stairs, opened the front door and went around the side of the house to get to the greenhouse.

After finding the window which was causing the problem, he fastened it and made his way back to the front of the house. Turning the corner, he saw that the front door was now closed.

"Oh great. The wind must have blown it shut."

Realising that he was still wearing his normal clothes, he rummaged through his pockets.

"Thank goodness for that," he said, when he found he had his keys. "Otherwise, I'd have definitely had no sleep this evening."

He went back up to his bedroom, this time changing into his pyjamas before getting into bed.

"It was lucky I had that key. Strange, though, how the door closed by itself. I've never known that to happen before. It must have been a strong gust of wind."

He yawned and waited for sleep to come, but it didn't. He looked at the light patterns made by the street lamps as they shone through the moving tree branches, onto the wall.

"Come on sleep, I'm bored lying here." But the harder he tried, the more awake he became. Sitting up in bed, he reached for a magazine, thinking it would help him to relax. It was then that he heard a muffled bump from downstairs.

He put the magazine down and listened carefully. There it was again. It wasn't a very loud sound, but there was definitely a distinctive bump which seemed to vibrate through the floor.

"There must be another window open downstairs and the draft is moving something round. It's not like mum to leave windows open at night, though. She's normally very careful." He climbed out of bed. "I'd better go and check. I'll make myself a drink while I'm down there."

He passed through the living room and into the kitchen. He switched on the fluorescent tube and waited for a few seconds while it flickered into life. Looking around the kitchen, he saw that one of the small windows had been left open.

"That's what was causing the problem." He

reached up and closed it.

Opening the fridge, he took out some cheese and poured himself a glass of orange juice. He carried them through to the front room, switched off the kitchen light and closed the door behind him. He sat down on the sofa and turned on the television.

Without any warning, there was a huge bang on the kitchen door. It was as if someone had hit it with a hammer. Mike stood up in fright, spilling his orange juice onto the carpet. There was the sound of a bottle rolling along the table then smashing onto the kitchen floor.

His whole body tingled with fear. There was no way he was going back into the kitchen. He just knew that the noise had not been caused by a gust of wind. There was something in there. Something which was strong, violent and evil.

Mike knew he had to get help. He ran upstairs and paused at the top to look back. There was a shadow at the bottom. Whatever was in the kitchen was now coming after him!

He ran into his parents' room. "Dad! Dad! Wake up! There's something downstairs!" He switched the light on and, to his horror, he saw that the bed was empty.

Rushing out, he went into his sister's room. "Kate, wake up!" he yelled. "Where are mum and dad?" He turned the lights on and again he saw that the bed was empty. The whole thing was uncanny.

There was a noise on the stairs; someone or

something was making its way up, slowly but surely. He ran into his own bedroom, locked the door and stood there shaking and shivering with fear. He was trapped.

He waited and listened. He could hear footsteps as they reached the landing and made their way towards his room. The door handle turned slowly. Whoever or whatever was outside was trying to get in. There was a huge bang on the door. Mike jumped back in fright. The thing outside was trying to force open the door. Mike picked up a chair and jammed it under the handle, hoping that it would wedge the door tight.

There was a loud splintering noise. Mike saw a long, knife blade slit through the door panel and begin to cut through the thin plywood. The sharp steel was withdrawn and he saw a hand reach in through the hole, feeling round for the door lock.

There was a click as the catch was taken off. The door handle turned again and the chair behind fell backwards onto the floor, as the thing forced its way in.

The blood drained from Mike's face as he saw that the attacker was entering the room. He looked round for something to defend himself with, but there was nothing. He picked up a pillow and held it in front of him as if that might prove to be some kind of defence.

Mike gasped as he recognised the person in front of him.

"Rob! Rob Murray! It was you all along! You're the one who tried to kill me in the car and made those threatening phone calls! It was you who chased me tonight. Why?"

Rob Murray stood staring. His face was twisted in a peculiar grimace. "Rachael. She's the reason." His voice sounded strange, as if it wasn't coming out of his mouth, but from somewhere else in the room. "Once I get rid of you, there will be no competition. She will be mine. You are going to DIE!"

The demented figure of Rob Murray advanced towards Mike, with the dagger raised in the air.

"No! Rob! You can't do this!" screamed Mike. He raised the pillow to cover his head.

He saw the wild eyes of a maniac as the knife slashed down towards his face.

Chapter 14
REVENGE

Mike sat up in bed with a start. He was covered in sweat and his heart was beating as if he had just run a marathon race. Leaping out of bed, he ran into his parents' bedroom. "You're here!" he exclaimed.

"Go away," Mr Campbell replied, pulling the covers over his shoulders. "It's only eight o'clock and it's Saturday."

Mike's mother sat up in bed. "What time did you come home last night?" she enquired.

"Yes," said his dad, deciding to join in the interrogation. "I came to pick you up at the arranged time and you weren't there. Someone said you had gone off with Angela. I hope you're not getting yourself into trouble. I expect you home at a reasonable time, not the middle of the night."

He was tempted to tell them about what happened on the way home, but if they were worried that someone was out to get him, he might be grounded, and that was the last thing he wanted.

"Okay, dad. I'll try to remember."

"I'm sure you will," replied Mr Campbell, not believing a word he was saying.

"So, it was all a nightmare," said Mike, as he climbed back into bed. "But what happened coming home from the party, wasn't. I'm sure it was Rob Murray. Who else could it be? He's the only one with the motive. Even in the nightmare, it was him and some people say that you should pay attention to what your dreams say. Well, I've got the message, and I'm going to fix Rob Murray once and for all. He's not going to come between Rachael and me. If he wants to play rough, then so will I!"

It wasn't until Monday morning, during school break, that Mike got the first opportunity to speak to Steve. Over the weekend, he had thought of nothing else except how he was going to get even with Rob Murray. Even thoughts of Rachael were pushed into the background as he fumed over what had happened at the party, and afterwards.

"Did you manage to get home from the party alright?" said Steve, as they sat down to share a packet of crisps.

Mike explained the terrifying events of the journey home while Steve listened, astounded.

"I'm convinced it was him who was following me."

"Well, why didn't you just stop and challenge him?"

"Would you challenge someone with a knife, on a dark country lane in the middle of the night? Come on, get real."

"I think you're right though," Steve

responded. "He *was* coming on strong with Rachael at the party, and he did finish up taking her home that night. You must have been really mad at him."

"He's also the one who locked me in the bathroom so he could get me out of the way. He doesn't like competition."

"Well, be fair, she did wait for you after your dad had left without you."

"Yes, but of all the people to go home with. I'd sooner that you had taken her home than Rob Murray."

Steve just smiled. "Have you seen her over the weekend?"

Mike pulled a face. "Do you think she's even going to speak to me after what happened? I hate that Rob Murray and I'm going to get even with him!"

"You're right," said Steve, in an encouraging voice. "You can't let him get away with it. You've got to choose the right moment, though. Wait till you've got the advantage, then stick one on him."

The bell rang for the end of break and everyone went off to their next lesson.

Mike couldn't concentrate in class. In fact, over the last few weeks, the quality of his work had deteriorated to the point where some teachers were threatening to send for his parents.

He chewed his pen and looked out of the window. His eyes opened wide as he saw Rob Murray walking across the playground towards the gymnasium, carrying a box. Mike knew that he must be taking the box to the history storeroom, which was round the back of the gym. He also knew that there were no classes in the gym for the next session and the place would be empty.

"*Choose your moment,*" he remembered Steve saying. This seemed to be as good a moment as any. He raised his arm to attract the teacher's attention.

"Yes?" asked the teacher.

"Can I go to the toilet, sir?"

"No you can't. You've only been in class for fifteen minutes. You should have gone at break-time."

"But I'm desperate, sir!" he said, standing up. "I've got to go now."

"Go on then, but next time please remember to go before you come into class."

Mike made his way out of the classroom, down the corridor and past the toilets. He ran across the playground towards the gym, keeping as close to the wall as possible so that he couldn't be seen from his classroom.

He opened the gym door, then made his way down another corridor which led to the storeroom. As he turned the corner, he could see Rob Murray unpacking the box of historical artefacts and placing them on the shelves. He was whistling a tune to himself.

"You're very happy today," Mike said, as he stopped and leaned against the wall.

Rob Murray turned round, startled. "What do you want? You're supposed to be in a maths lesson."

"I want to know what's going on with you and Rachael and why you're always butting into my business. You locked me in the bathroom at the Hallowe'en party so that you could take Rachael home. What's your game?"

Rob put the box down. "Listen thick-head. You're the one who left Rachael standing. What did you expect her to do, walk home on her own in the dark? I did you a favour. If you don't know how to treat a girl, then that's just your bad luck. And as for locking you in the bathroom - that had nothing to do with me."

"Come off it. That was part of your plan. As soon as I went for a drink, you were dancing with her. Then you made sure I was out of the way."

Rob said nothing, but put the box down and attempted to push his way past Mike who was now standing in the middle of the corridor. "Move out of my way!" he said brusquely. "Or you might find yourself grovelling on the floor like last time!"

"You got lucky last time," said Mike, standing in front of him defiantly.

Rob lurched forward towards Mike, but this time he was ready and moved to one side,

94

sending him sprawling on the floor. Rob got to his feet and came charging forwards with the intention of knocking Mike off balance but, again, he was too quick and stepped back, catching Rob with a glancing blow. As Rob stood up for the next attack, Mike decided to take the initiative, and before Rob could steady himself, he landed two quick punches. Rob went crashing back into the history storeroom, knocking the contents of the artefacts box onto the floor.

Mike stood his ground waiting for Rob to come forward again. He felt confident that this time he was going to win and make Murray pay for what he had done.

"Come on!" he taunted, "Or have you had enough yet?"

As Rob lay on the ground he thought he was going to be beaten. He felt around on the floor for something which he might use as a weapon, and his hand closed upon the handle of a knife. He looked and saw it was the replica, decorated, Anglo Saxon knife that they had been using in the last history lesson. It must have been knocked off the shelf when the fight first started.

Rob rose from the floor, slowly, keeping it behind his back. He moved towards Mike who was waiting for him. Mike was just about to leap forward when Rob pulled the knife from its hiding place, and pushed it towards his enemy. Mike stopped and drew back. He was suddenly very afraid.

"So, it was you who was following me home last night. You're very handy with a knife. I can see that."

Rob just laughed. "Not so brave now, are you?" he said, moving forward all the time.

Mike retreated down the corridor. He was afraid and he could see that Rob was very angry. He stopped when he reached the wall. He could go no further.

Rob moved closer towards Mike until he held the dagger close to his face. Mike clenched his fist ready for action, but what was he going to do? Should he try to fight his way out of the situation? He looked into Rob's eyes and decided not to. To fight someone with a knife was just asking for trouble.

So, he just stood there, motionless, as Rob brandished the knife in front of his face.

"You've got a problem!" Rob said scornfully. "Twice now you've tried it on with me and twice you've come off the worst. Wise up and keep out of my way!"

He moved back down the corridor holding the knife in front of him with his eyes fixed on Mike. "Don't move!" he said, as he retreated. When he reached the store, he tossed the knife into the box and made a quick exit.

School had just finished and Mike was

standing by the gate talking to Steve. "I can't believe it. That's twice he's humiliated me. Every time I've tried to fix him, he's come out on top. What have I got to do to teach him a lesson?"

"Don't worry, you'll get the better of him next time," said Steve. "You've got to do something because he's going to make you a laughing stock in front of Rachael. That's his plan - to make you look like a fool who can't sort out his problems."

"He's crafty alright. He seems to know my every move."

"Look - there he is now," said Steve, pointing across the road.

Mike looked over, feelings of revenge and jealousy festering inside him. "I think I'll follow him and see where he's going to. See you later, Steve."

He crossed the road and kept a long distance behind Rob. He soon realised that Rob was heading into town. He continued to follow, determined that he was going to find a way to get back at his enemy. He had tried the direct approach twice and that hadn't been very successful. A more subtle method was needed.

Just before he reached the town centre, Rob crossed some waste ground and then passed under a high walkway which led into Main Street. He passed the supermarket, stopped outside a barber's shop and looked at the products on display before going in.

"He must be having a haircut. He could be at

least half an hour in there," Mike thought.

Opposite was a McDonald's take-away, so Mike decided to go in and have a coke while he waited.

He bought his drink and went to sit down at a table, a little way back from the window.

At that moment, he saw Zilla pass by in the street. He turned his face away, but it was too late - she had seen him. Stopping, she tapped on the window and gave a wave. Mike smiled back weakly.

"Go away, Zilla," he thought, as he saw her opening the door.

"Hi! Fancy meeting you here," she said cheerfully. "I see you're on your own. Mind if I come and join you?" She looked deeply into his eyes as she sat down.

"I'm just doing a bit of shopping," he lied, looking away from her piercing gaze.

"Did you know that Rachael was very upset about the party? She said she doesn't want to see you again."

Mike looked up angrily. "It wasn't my fault. That idiot Rob Murray locked me in the bathroom. By the time I managed to get out, she was gone."

Zilla seemed quite pleased. "There's a disco on in town next Saturday," she said, touching his hand gently. "Would you like to go?"

Mike saw the door of the barber's shop open. "Yes, that would be nice," he said, not thinking what he was saying. He watched as Rob came out and walked off down the street.

"I'll have to go, Zilla. I'll see you later."

"But you haven't finished your coke!" she shouted after him. "Mike? I'll call round to your house on Saturday!"

Mike ran across the street and turned off down a side road. He had an idea.

He raced on until he came to the piece of waste land he had crossed earlier, and picked up a brick that he found on the ground. Next, he sprinted as fast as he could up the steps which led to the walkway. He knew that Rob would be passing this way in a few moments.

"He's scared me once too often; now it's my turn to give him a fright."

Mike's intention was to drop the brick near Rob as he walked under the walkway. Peeping over the edge, he could see Rob approaching. There was no one else around.

"This is perfect. I'll drop it well away from him, but close enough to give him a fright. He won't mess with me again."

Chapter 15
THE LAUGHING MAN

As soon as the brick left his hand, Mike realised that he had made a stupid mistake. "This is crazy. I could kill someone doing this."

"Watch out!" he shouted, over the edge. Crouching down by the wall of the walkway he buried his face in his hands, praying that the brick would not hit Rob. He had thrown it well away from where he was walking, but suppose he suddenly changed direction?

There was a brittle crack as the brick hit the pavement and shattered into fragments. Mike gave a huge sigh of relief. He knew that no one had been injured.

"Who did that?" he heard Rob calling from below. He daren't look over the edge or he would be recognised.

There was a sound of someone running and he realised that Rob was sprinting up the steps towards where he was hiding. Mike stood up and ran in the opposite direction, but he knew that Rob would be up to the top in a few seconds and he might see him. He ducked into a small alley. A few moments later, he heard Rob come running past.

As soon as he was out of sight, Mike retraced his steps and made his way down into Main Street. He was angry, but this time his anger was directed against himself. "That must be the

BAD BLOOD

most stupid thing I've ever done in my life. I must have been crazy to think of such a thing."

When Mike arrived home, the house was empty. He was putting away his school bag when the phone rang. After switching on the tape recorder at the side of the phone, he picked up the receiver.

"Hello?" he said nervously.

"Hi, Mike - this is Rachael."

"Rachael!" Mike exclaimed. "I haven't spoken to you since the party."

"That's what I'm phoning about. I was really annoyed when I couldn't find you and thought you must have gone off with someone else. I was talking to your cousin, Angela and she told me that you were both locked in the bathroom. So I realise it wasn't your fault. I'm sorry I've been avoiding you."

"It was that Rob Murray who did it. He took you home, didn't he?"

"I had no choice, Mike. I was on my own, and I was also fed up with you because I thought you'd gone without me. I did wait for you."

Mike was silent for a moment. He realised that he would have to be careful what he said, otherwise they would finish up having an argument and that was the last thing he wanted.

"I'll see you then, Mike. I just wanted you to know I'm not angry with you."

"No - don't go yet," said Mike, trying to think quickly. "Would you like to come for a drive on Saturday evening?"

"Yes, that would be nice," she replied. "I'll get my dad to bring me over to your house at eight o'clock."

"All I need is a car," said Mike to himself, as he completed the last question of his homework. There was no point in asking his dad, but there was someone else with a car that he knew. Angela was coming round later that evening to see Kate. She might take some persuading after what had happened last time, but he was quite confident that he could do it.

He opened the cupboard in his room and took out a box of chocolates that he had intended to give to Rachael. "These will do to begin with."

Later on that evening, Mike came into the living room where Kate and Angela were talking.

"These are for you, Angela," he said, handing her the box of chocolates.

"It's not my birthday. What have I done to deserve this?" Angela looked at him suspiciously. "You want something don't you? That's the only time you're ever nice to me.

Isn't it?"

Mike nodded and said nothing.

"Well? Ask me, then," Angela prompted, curious about the favour he wanted.

"Can I borrow your car on Saturday, please?"

Angela gave a grunt of indignation. "Borrow the car! After what you did last time? Putting the car into reverse gear instead of first. You don't think I'm going to entrust my car to you do you?" she said, as she opened the chocolates and offered one to Kate.

"Please, Angela. It's very important."

"So's my car," retorted Angela, biting into a rum truffle.

"I'll owe you one."

"And it'll be a very big one," she answered. "These chocolates are only for starters."

"I promise I'll drive really carefully."

Mike could see that things were going his way but it was obvious it was going to cost him a hefty price.

"I'll get my dad to drop me off with the car on Saturday. Kate and I are going down town to the disco."

"Yep," he smirked to himself as he closed the door and went back to his room. "I can really twist those girls round my little finger."

☠

On Saturday, Angela's dad brought her to the house and left the car for Mike to use. Angela and Kate were in the bathroom getting ready to go to the disco when there was a knock on the door.

"Surely this can't be Rachael? She's not due here till eight o'clock," said Mike, looking at his watch. The time was seven-thirty.

He opened the door ready to greet Rachael. "Zilla!" he said, with his voice full of surprise.

"You haven't forgotten have you?" she said, as she walked into the house. "You said we were going to the disco tonight."

Mike thought hard, then he remembered. He was sitting in McDonald's, drinking coke, waiting for Rob to come out of the barber's shop when Zilla had joined him. It must have been then that he'd made the arrangement, or at least she thought they had. He couldn't remember exactly what he had said to Zilla because he had been busy watching for Rob, and hadn't been listening properly.

"I can see you're ready then," she said, looking at Mike who was dressed up in his best clothes to meet Rachael.

"Would you like a coffee?" Mike said, playing for time.

"Yes, please," said Zilla.

Mike went into the kitchen and leaned against the cupboard door. "Why is nothing ever straightforward?" he moaned to himself. "Rachael will be arriving in a few minutes. What will she say if she thinks I've asked Zilla to go to a disco? I'll have to tell her, but it's going to be so embarrassing."

He returned to the living room with the coffee.

"Zilla," he began, but didn't finish, because Kate and Angela had just walked into the room.

"Zilla. What are you doing here?" asked Kate.

"I'm going to the disco with Mike," she said, smiling sweetly.

"But I thought you were going out with..."

"With the guys. That's right. I'm sorry Zilla," he said, turning towards her, "But I'd forgotten I'd already arranged to go bowling with the boys from school."

"Well, why didn't you let me know?" replied Zilla, looking hurt.

"Well, I thought you could go to the disco with Angela and Kate. They're leaving shortly. Aren't you?" he said, looking pointedly at Kate.

Angela suppressed a giggle, but said nothing.

"Come on - let's go, Zilla," said Kate glaring at Mike. "You're better off with us."

Mike breathed a sigh of relief as he saw them walking off to catch the bus. Two minutes later, Rachael arrived, driven by her father.

"I've not seen much of my friend Zilla recently," Rachael mused, as she and Mike pulled away from the kerb in Angela's car.

Mike just gulped and said nothing.

"Should we go to the disco?" she continued, enthusiastically.

"No - I think we'll go to the cinema instead," replied Mike.

"That was a lovely evening," said Rachael, as the car came to a stop outside her house. Mike leaned back in his seat. Everything had gone perfectly and he felt happy. He really got on well with Rachael and all the unpleasant things that had happened seemed to be fading into the past. Even Rob Murray didn't seem to be that much of a threat anymore. Mike moved closer to Rachael and put his arm round her.

"I've really enjoyed this evening, Rachael."

"So have I," she said, looking closely into his eyes and taking a long deep breath.

A sharp, cackling laugh broke through the calm of the night. Rachael lifted her head from Mike's shoulder, startled by the strange noise.

"What's that?" she said, suddenly afraid.

Mike looked along the darkened street but nothing moved. The cackling laugh stopped for a moment, then started again. Mike opened the car door and stood on the pavement. He clenched his fist ready for something to happen. He wasn't going to be taken by surprise again and was determined nothing was going to hurt Rachael. The hysterical laughing continued. Mike listened carefully. It seemed to be coming from behind the car. He bent down and looked underneath, to see if anyone was hiding at the back.

"It seems to be coming from inside the car."

"How can it be ?" said Rachael, unnerved by the weird, uncanny voice.

Mike slowly made his way round to the back of the car. The sound had stopped. When it started again, he realised where it was coming from.

"Rachael!" he said apprehensively. "There's someone in the boot of the car!"

Chapter 16
NIGHT FRIGHT

"The boot's unlocked. Someone must have crept in when the car was parked," Mike whispered.

"What shall we do?" said Rachael quietly.

"Is this the maniac who has been following me?" thought Mike, as he put his hands on the boot lock, ready to open it. "Even Rob Murray doesn't laugh like that."

He turned the lock and flung the boot open, prepared for anything. Rachael stood back, nervously biting her fingers in anticipation.

Mike bent down and picked something up. "Look at this," he said, giving it to Rachael.

"It's a battery toy." She turned it round in her hand and watched as the figure of a man moved back and forth, cackling hysterically.

Mike laughed at his own fearfulness. "It's one of Angela's gadgets. It must have rolled onto its start button when we stopped. Wait till I see her."

The door of Rachael's house opened and someone looked out. "That's my mum checking up on me. Thanks for a lovely evening, Mike. I'll see you soon," she said, as she waved goodbye.

The next day, Mike called round to Steve's house. He was eager to tell him the good news about Rachael.

"Hi, Steve," he said as he opened the door.

"What's new?" Steve asked, as they sat down in the living room.

"I saw Rachael again last night," said Mike, beaming with pleasure. "We've made things up and everything is back on track again."

"That's great," said Steve in a dull voice.

"You're looking a bit fed up. Why don't you try to get out a bit more?" said Mike, helpfully. Suddenly he had an idea. He was still feeling a bit guilty at the way he had treated Zilla the other evening, and he had been thinking about how he could make amends.

"Steve - how would you like to make up a foursome tonight? Me and Rachael and you and Zilla. I could borrow the car and we could all go down town."

"Zilla?" said Steve, surprised by the suggestion. "You must be kidding."

"She's not that bad," said Mike, defending Zilla. "In fact, I think she's quite pretty. She seems to have changed recently. I always thought she was rather plain and dull, but now I think she's quite attractive. If I wasn't tied up with Rachael, I'd probably ask her myself."

Steve pulled his face. "Zilla, she has that funny cough." He shook his head. "Have you sorted Rob Murray out yet?" he asked, changing the subject.

"That's all in the past. I think he's got the message and won't be causing any more trouble," said Mike, not wanting to tell Steve about the brick-dropping incident.

The evening passed quickly. They watched a video and had a chat about school. "I'd better be going home, it's getting late," said Mike looking at his watch.

"I've been thinking about that foursome plan you mentioned earlier," said Steve. "Maybe it's not such a bad idea after all. It could be good fun."

Mike looked at Steve, surprised that he had changed his mind after being so dismissive when he had first made the suggestion.

"I'll contact Zilla and you could pick us both up from here tomorrow."

"That sounds great," said Mike, pleased that Steve was coming out. "I'll see you tomorrow then."

Angela screamed with laughter when Mike told her about the toy in the boot. "That will teach you not to borrow my car."

"Talking of borrowing the car…"

"Okay," she said, without any further persuasion. "I suppose someone may as well make use of it until I pass my test. But you'll have to collect it yourself from my house."

"Thanks, Angela. You're an angel," said

Mike, giving her a peck on the cheek.

The following evening, Mike and Rachael arrived at Steve's house. Zilla and Steve were waiting by the door as the car drew up.

Zilla just nodded a greeting as she climbed into the car and gave Mike a glowering look.

"There's a new ice-cream parlour opening down on Main Street," Mike said, as he pulled into the car park. "We could call in there and decide what to do for the rest of the evening."

"Sounds like a great idea," said Steve enthusiastically.

They walked round the corner into Main Street towards the ice-cream parlour. "Hang on a moment," said Steve, putting his hand into his pocket. "I think I've left my money on the seat of the car."

"Let's go back and get it," said Rachael.

"Just give me the keys and I'll run back. I won't be long."

Steve arrived back within five minutes.

"We've got you an ice-cream," said Mike, pushing a huge peach melba towards him.

"This looks delicious."

"How about taking a ride to Billinge Hill when we've finished? There's a really good view from the top," suggested Mike, in between mouthfuls of sweet peach syrup.

"I don't think we'll bother. We've decided to go to the cinema on our own, haven't we Zilla?" said Steve, turning towards her.

"That's right," answered Zilla, casting her eyes down, towards her ice-cream.

"But I thought we were all going to do something together?" said Mike, disappointed.

"Mike - they want to be on their own. That's okay, isn't it?" said Rachael

"I suppose so," Mike replied, surprised by Steve's sudden change of heart.

They all finished their ice-creams and said goodbye. "I can't understand him," said Mike as he started the car. "Why did he change his mind? He was all for it yesterday."

"I don't mind," said Rachael, moving closer. "It means we've got more time together."

"That's true," he said, smiling.

It was a beautiful evening and the sun was quite low in the sky as they drove out towards Billinge Hill. They stopped at the top where there was a small car park, and watched the sun as it dipped below the horizon.

"I wish life could always be this beautiful," murmured Mike, who was enjoying the serenity of the evening.

"It's getting quite chilly, now that the sun has gone down," observed Rachael, pulling up the collar of her coat. "Can we go?"

"Let's drive back into town," suggested

Mike. "I'm getting hungry. Perhaps we could get a pizza?"

He drove out of the car park. The road was flat for the first hundred yards, then the hill started. As they approached, Rachael read the warning sign. "Steep hill. Keep in low gear."

Mike was in fourth gear by the time he reached the top of the hill and the car began to pick up speed as it started down the steep gradient. He changed down into third gear, but as the car continued to accelerate approaching the first bend, he had to press gently on the brake.

Instantly, he knew that there was something seriously wrong. "Oh no!" he shouted. "The brake pedal has gone right down to the floor and nothing is happening. There's no way we can stop!"

Chapter 17
LUCKY TO BE ALIVE

As they hit the bend, their speed was rapidly increasing.

"Change down to second gear!" shouted Rachael, as she realised they were in desperate trouble.

Mike kept a tight grip on the steering wheel, not daring even to change gear for fear he might lose control of the car altogether.

The car tyres squealed as the vehicle careered around the bend and reached a straight part of the road. Mike was about to throw the car into second gear, but saw that the road had narrowed to a single track, and there was a car coming up directly in front of them. He sounded his horn and flashed his lights at the other car, which veered over into the ditch to avoid Mike, who was now hurtling down the hill at a tremendous speed.

As quickly as he could, he pressed the clutch and put the engine into second gear. There was a metallic crunching and a smell of burning oil as the gears engaged and turned the engine at a ferocious rate. The rev. counter on the dashboard shot into the red zone, but the car didn't appear to slow very much.

Instead, it lurched onwards down the hill, rapidly approaching a second bend.

"Pull the hand brake!" Mike yelled out to

Rachael, realising that if they didn't slow down on the bend, they would smash into the drystone wall on the edge of the road.

Rachael pulled the brake but it seemed to make very little difference. "Use two hands!" he screamed as the car went into the bend. She managed to yank the brake on a couple more notches before she was thrown over against the passenger door.

He just got around the bend without flying off the road when he saw a large sign. "Temporary traffic lights. STOP HERE WHEN THE SIGN SHOWS RED."

A car was stopped directly in their path, waiting for the lights to change. Mike's car was now slowing down but he knew there was no possibility of stopping before he hit the stationary car in the rear. He changed down into first gear.

Rachael covered her face as the car raced towards the waiting vehicle. Seconds before impact, the lights changed and the car in front moved off.

"We've done it!" Mike shouted with joy. Once through the lights the car continued to slow down and eventually they ground to a halt.

For a few moments they both sat saying nothing. Rachael was furious but relieved.

"Mike! What is going on? Everytime I see you, something terrible happens. I can't take any more of this!" She put her head down and burst into tears.

"I thought all this was over, but it's still happening. I'm sure it's Rob Murray."

"Oh give it a rest! You blame him for everything!" said Rachael, angrily. "Let's go and find a phone!"

"Dad? Can you come out and pick us up? We've almost had a terrible accident and the car isn't safe to drive." All they could do was wait.

It wasn't long before Mike saw his father's B.M.W. approaching, followed shortly afterwards by the flashing lights of an AA rescue van.

"The brakes failed as we started down the hill," Mike explained.

"Then you're lucky to be alive. It's a dangerous road to come down, even if everything is working properly."

The AA man knelt down on the ground to look under the car. "There's probably a leak in the brake pipe and you've lost fluid." He shone the light under the car. "This is unbelievable!" he exclaimed. "Someone has deliberately cut clean through your brake pipe. It was certainly no accident. I think you should inform the police."

The AA mechanic agreed to tow the car to the nearest garage while Mr Campbell took Rachael and Mike home.

When he reached Rachael's house, Mike helped her out of the car. Her face was white and she looked as if she might faint. "I won't be a moment, dad. I'm just seeing Rachael to the door."

"Rachael, when can I see you again?" he asked.

"Mike - I like you very much and I'm very fond of you, but you're a very dangerous person to be around. I know someone is out to get you, but I can't take the risk any more. We could have both been killed tonight, and that's not the first time it's happened. I don't want to see you for the time being. Maybe when this is all over, we could try again."

"Rachael."

"I'm sorry, Mike." She turned away and walked towards the house. She was crying.

☠

The next day, Mike phoned Steve.

"Hi," said Steve, cheerily. "Did you enjoy yourselves last night? We did. I think Zilla's quite struck on me, actually."

"It's just as well you didn't come with us, or you might not be here now. Someone cut through the brake pipes and the brakes failed completely as we came down that steep section of Billinge Hill."

Steve whistled down the phone. "That's really serious, Mike. Someone is out to get you. Do you think it was Rob Murray?"

"I thought so at first, but Rachael thinks I'm

wrong to be blaming him for everything."

"Well, I think he's the most likely candidate. Who else is there?"

"I suppose it could be someone else, but I can't think of anyone who has a grudge against me."

"How's Rachael taking it?"

"It's over. She doesn't want to see me again. She says I'm too dangerous to be with. I'm really cheesed off."

There was a ring at the doorbell. "I'll see you later, Steve - there's someone at the door."

"Zilla," said Mike, surprised. "Come on in. If you want to see Kate, I'm afraid she's out."

Zilla sat down in the chair. She gave a little cough before she began to speak. "It's you I've come to see, Mike - not Kate. I heard about your near-accident last night. It must have been a terrible shock. How are you feeling?"

"It was awful," said Mike, glad that he had someone to talk to. "I'm really fed up because Rachael said that she doesn't want to see me anymore. That's almost as bad as what happened with the car."

"Rachael told me you weren't seeing each other again."

"She told you that?" said Mike, annoyed that Rachael had been talking behind his back.

"Yes. That's one of the reasons why I wanted to see you." She stood up and went to sit next to Mike on the sofa. "Mike," she said moving closer. "You and I get on very well together, don't we? So, why don't we start seeing more of each other? Now that Rachael doesn't want to see you again, what's to stop you?"

Mike was taken by surprise. "But I thought you had something going with Steve?" He was about to tell her what Steve had said on the phone, but decided not to.

"Whatever gave you that idea? We went out together last night but there's nothing in that. No, Mike - what do you think about us?" she said, softly placing her hand on his.

"What about all the sinister things happening to me? Doesn't that bother you?"

"No."

Mike was embarrassed and didn't know what to do. It was true he did like Zilla and he found her attractive.

"Zilla, I am fond of you, but it's just too soon. I need some time to get over Rachael. I can't just switch off like that."

Zilla stood up. "Alright, Mike. Perhaps another time."

The phone rang and Mike swooped it up, half hoping it would be Rachael. "Hello?" There was an ominous silence on the other end of the phone. "Not again," Mike thought as he pressed the button on his recording machine.

Chapter 18
MIKE AND ZILLA

A crackling, rasping voice echoed down the telephone line.

"You were lucky with the car, but you won't be so lucky next time. And there will be a next time."

Mike handed the phone to Zilla so that she could listen. She held it against her ear, saying nothing. Then the line went dead.

Zilla put the phone down. "It's horrible," she said, casting her eyes down to the floor and shaking her head. "Mike," she said, pleading. "Can't you forget about Rachael?"

"No, Zilla. I'm sorry. It's too soon."

Zilla said goodbye and left Mike on his own.

The next day, Mike woke up with a bad headache. "What am I going to do today?" he sighed. "No Rachael. No fun. No nothing. My life is complete misery."

"I hear that Rachael has packed you in," chirped Kate as she bounced into the room.

"How did you know that? It's none of your business," he responded gruffly.

"News travels fast in this part of the world. Anyway, I don't know why you're looking so glum. It's not the end of the world. Stop feeling sorry for yourself and do something about it."

He was just about to give an angry reply when he stopped and considered. "She's right. Why should I sit moping in the house all day?"

After breakfast he phoned Steve.

"Hi there, buddy! How about you and me go bowling tonight? Or maybe we could get a few of the guys together like we used to and have a bit of fun."

"Sorry, Mike, but I've already arranged with my parents to visit some relatives out of town. If I'd known earlier I could have come."

Mike put the phone down feeling fed up again. "I could go out with Kate and Angela, but that's not much fun," he thought, as he flicked through his address book. "What about Zilla? Zilla... No, on second thoughts, perhaps not," he chuckled to himself.

Why not Zilla? A voice in his head echoed her name.

Mike thought again. He did quite like Zilla, though sometimes she could be a bit of a pain.

"Anything's better than sitting home alone," he told himself as he dialled her number.

"Hi? Zilla?"

"Is that you Mike?" she said, surprised by his call.

"Would you like to come out with me tonight?" he said.

"But I thought you said you need time to get over Rachael."

"Well, I've had two hours! That's long

enough isn't it? Seriously, do you want to call round at my house later on?"

"Alright," said Zilla, trying not to sound too enthusiastic.

☠

Mike watched Zilla through the window walking up the garden path.

"Perhaps I've misjudged her in the past," he thought to himself. "She's quite an attractive girl, really."

☠

Several hours later, they returned to Mike's house. It was obvious to Kate as she opened the door that they had had a very enjoyable evening.

"Hello, Zilla. I didn't know you were seeing Mike tonight."

"We really enjoyed ourselves, didn't we, Mike?" she said, with a sense of satisfaction, as she walked, beaming into the living room.

"Didn't take you long to overcome your grief, did it?" Kate hissed at Mike as he walked past.

"Only taking your advice," he replied, as he followed Zilla into the room.

"I'll leave you two alone," said Kate loudly, and she disappeared upstairs.

Mike went into the kitchen to make some tea when the phone rang. "Would you answer that please, Zilla? I won't be a moment."

When he returned, carrying two cups, he saw that Zilla was still talking on the phone.

"We've had a lovely evening. We went to the cinema and then Mike took me to a Chinese restaurant." She paused. "Somebody wants to speak to you," she whispered, handing the phone to him.

"Hello? Mike speaking," he said, wondering who Zilla was talking to.

"It's Rachael, Mike. I hear you've had a very nice evening out with Zilla. I was phoning up to say that we could still call each other and keep in contact even though we're not seeing each other, but obviously you've made other plans."

"Wait! Rachael!" Mike cried, but the phone had gone dead.

"What did she say?" asked Zilla, knowing perfectly well how the conversation had ended.

Mike felt sick and guilty. He kicked himself for betraying the trust of someone who was very important to him.

"Forget about Rachael, Mike. She's in the past. Let's think about us," whispered Zilla. She moved closer.

"I think it's time I took you home - it's getting late," said Mike, looking at his watch.

Fifteen minutes later, they arrived outside Zilla's house. Mike was feeling miserable and wanted to get back home as quickly as possible.

Zilla obviously had other plans.

"Mike," she said, drawing him towards her and gazing deeply into his eyes.

Mike drew back. "No Zilla," he turned and walked away.

"You're a fool, Mike Campbell!" she shouted after him angrily. "A stupid fool!"

Mike walked off, oblivious to what she was saying. All he could think of was Rachael and how he had let her down.

He had only been home for ten minutes when the phone rang. "I'm not going to answer that. It will be Zilla." The phone continued ringing. "But it could be Rachael."

He pressed his record button then picked up the phone.

There was an empty silence.

"Your time is running out," the voice crackled. Mike slammed the phone down and unplugged it from the socket.

He flopped down onto the settee, both angry and miserable. He had lost Rachael. He had had enough of the phone calls and threats to his life.

"There must be something I can do. Some clue that I've overlooked. I've got to find out who's doing this, because I can't take much more."

Chapter 19
GHOST TRAIN

The next morning when Mike woke, there was only one thing on his mind. He had to find an answer. There must be some way I can hit back, he thought, as he opened the porch door and picked up the mail. He had been awake for half the night trying to think of a solution to his problem, but he hadn't come up with any answers.

He placed the letters on the table, went to the cupboard and took out some bread to make toast. As he ate his breakfast, he looked through the mail. Nothing for me - just bills and circulars, he thought, and put them to one side.

"Maybe I'd better just check the telephone bill," he said, as he picked up the top letter. The previous month, both he and Kate had been in hot water because of the size of the bill, and Mr Campbell had threatened to have a lock put on the phone if it happened again.

As he pulled out the bill, a piece of paper fell onto the floor. It was an advert from the phone company for new services and products.

"Look at this," he whispered to himself, reading the words in front of him. "Dial 1471 after the last call you receive and you will be able to find out the number of the caller."

Mike completely forget about his intention

to check the bill. "This is brilliant. It's exactly what I need." Just at that moment Kate walked into the room. "Kate. Did you know that you can trace a phone call if you dial 1471?"

"Of course I did. Everyone knows that. It's been out for ages."

"Well, why didn't you tell me?" said Mike, with a tone of annoyance.

"I never thought about it," she said casually, as she popped a slice of bread into the toaster.

"Kate," he said excitedly, "this could be the answer to my problem. Next time it happens, I'll just dial 1471 and have the caller traced."

"That's alright if it comes from a house phone, but what if it comes from a call-box? By the time you get there, the person calling will be well gone."

Mike pulled a face. He hadn't thought about that.

"And what if they call while you're out?" she continued negatively.

Mike thought carefully. "The first thing I'm going to do is get a list from the phone company, of the numbers and addresses of all the local, public phones. Then when the call comes through, at least I'll have something to go on."

"Mmm... that's a good idea," Kate answered as she buttered her toast.

Mike was ecstatic. At last he felt like he was doing something useful. Now he had a chance of fighting back. "Kate, will you help me on this?"

"Okay," she said, without taking her eyes off the local paper she was reading.

"I'm going to ask dad if I can borrow his mobile phone. If the call comes while I'm out, you could dial 1471 then ring through to me and let me know the number straight away."

"Sure," she repeated. Her attention was elsewhere. "Mike, have you seen this?" she said, referring to the newspaper. "It says that there's going to be a funfair set up on that piece of waste ground by the town centre. I could ask Angela if she'd like to come and we could all go together. What do you think?"

"That sounds like a good idea," he said. "But I'm not sure if I'll be able to. I've got a lot of homework to catch up on. They're coming down heavy on me at school. Mum and dad are going to be called in if I don't get some work done."

"Why not do it in the library this afternoon and meet us at the fairground in the evening when you've finished? It's right across the road from the library."

Mike thought that was a good idea. "Alright. We'll do that."

Mike wasn't used to spending a whole afternoon working, but this was an emergency and he would be able to have some fun at the fairground later on.

"Kate - I'm taking the mobile phone with me. Remember to contact me straight away if there's a phone call. And don't forget to press the record button before you answer. I'm logging all the calls."

"Okay. I'll see you at seven-thirty."

The library was open late and Mike found that by seven o'clock, his concentration was beginning to wander. Never mind - he was almost finished. It was getting dark outside and he could see the reflection of the fairground lights on the ceiling of the library. He yawned and stretched his arms. Just at that moment, the mobile phone in his bag began to ring.

"Shhhh," he heard the librarian reprimand him from behind her desk.

He pulled out the phone and answered as quietly as he could. "Is that you Kate?"

"Yes!" she answered in an excited voice. "There's been another call. I dialled 1471 and I've got the number here."

She read it down the phone as Mike quickly made a note. He scanned through the list of telephone numbers and addresses that he got from the phone company earlier in the day.

"I've found it," he said, in a hushed tone. "The call came from a phone booth in Hall Street."

"Hall Street! That's right by the fairground! You could probably see it from the library window."

Mike was excited. "You're right. I'm going to

have a look. I'll see you later."

"Mike - don't do anything stupid," Kate implored, in an agitated voice.

Putting the phone back into his bag, Mike walked over to the window. It was almost dark outside and he had to cup his hands against the glass to see properly. The call-box was on the corner of the road and he could see someone was just leaving the booth, but it was too dark to make out who it was.

He scooped his belongings up into his bag and sprinted for the door. It mightn't even be the right person, he thought, as he swept through the swing doors into the street. He could see the person who had been in the booth was now making his way into the funfair.

"I hope I don't lose him in the crowd," Mike gasped, as he chased after him. He thought he recognised the man from the back, as the same person he had chased from the bridge, but it was difficult to be certain.

The dark figure turned for a moment looking back towards the library. Mike slowed down, hoping he wouldn't look too conspicuous as he wanted to take the man by surprise.

It was too late. The man paused, looked at him then took off like a rocket. Mike raced after him again as fast as he could. This might be his only chance and he didn't want to blow it.

The stranger disappeared around the corner into the funfair; it was another twenty seconds before Mike reached the bend. He stopped and looked around. The whole area was brightly illuminated, but he couldn't see any sign of a man running.

"I've lost him. He could be anywhere."

Mike calculated how long it would take to cross to the other side of the fairground. "He must still be here. He didn't have time to go very far."

Directly opposite to where he was standing he could see the ghost train. One of the carriages was just about to enter the ride. "That's him!" shouted Mike, triumphantly. "He's going into the ghost ride."

By the time he had reached the turnstile, the carriage had disappeared. He pushed past the attendant hoping to jump on the next train, but a hand grabbed him from behind. "Hang on you! You haven't paid!"

Mike fumbled in his pocket for some money. "Wait a moment," he said to himself. "There's no other way out. I can just sit here and catch him as he comes through."

He waited, watching each person who came out of the ride. Even though he hadn't seen the man's face, he was quite sure he would recognise him. After five minutes, nothing had happened.

He must still be in there. He's probably guessed that I'd be waiting out here for him.

"One ticket please," said Mike as he handed over the money. He had decided that his only option was to go on the ride himself. There was a possibility the man would come out as he went in, but that was a risk he had to take.

The carriage lurched forwards and barged through a set of rubber doors. It was a long time since he had been on a ghost train and if it hadn't been for the predicament he was in, he would have enjoyed the ride.

The train rumbled on through a tunnel painted in lurid colours, strange moaning and groaning noises coming from all around him. Directly ahead was a brick wall painted with a huge skeleton. It appeared that the train would crash into the wall, but at the last moment it swerved at a right angle and continued in a different direction.

He could be anywhere in here. There are hundreds of places to hide. Where am I going to find him? He considered climbing off the slow-moving train but then decided that that probably wasn't a good idea.

The narrow tunnel widened into a large cave and a ghostly figure in a white garment stood on the track just a few metres ahead. As the train approached, the arms of the ghost opened, revealing a large dagger in its hand. Mike ducked as the carriage appeared to hit the ghost, but a second before contact was made, it whisked up into the air above his head, out of sight. A loud banshee wail issued from the disappearing ghoul.

Mike took a deep breath; his heart was beating fast. "This is no place for the fainthearted, especially as there could be a real psycho on the loose."

The carriage made another sharp right turn which brought it into the next cavern. Ahead, Mike could see a grey figure dressed like a monk, holding a huge scythe in its hand. A white skull with hollow eyes peered from underneath its cowl.

What does this one do? thought Mike, preparing himself for another fright. The train approached the evil-looking monk and Mike braced himself, ready for something to happen. He lowered his head expecting some deadly object to come flying in his direction. It was then that he noticed there was a plastic dummy lying at the side of the track. The dummy was fixed in a pose that was very similar to the fast-approaching mad monk.

Awful thoughts flashed across his mind. Has someone taken the dummy's clothes off? Is that a real person standing in front of me? He looked closely at the masked figure which was now only one metre away. He thought he saw a twinkle of reflected light from the eyes behind the mask.

He watched the arm of the grey clad figure draw back and raise its huge scythe above its head. The second the blade moved forward, Mike realised that it was meant for him. Instinctively, he ducked and heard a silky swish as the curved metal skimmed across the surface of his head. He fell sideways out of the carriage, crashing his head against the side of the rail. A trickle of warm blood flowed down his face and into his mouth. He instantly rolled to one side in case the now unseen figure made another attempt to separate his head from his body. He heard a noise and looked up, but the hooded man had disappeared and he didn't know in which direction.

Mike was petrified. All he wanted to do now was to find a way out before the crazed monk attacked him again. There was a rumble from further down the track and the next train appeared carrying two children.

"Please tell the attendant to come in and help me! There's a maniac hiding somewhere inside here! He wants to kill me!" Mike shouted, as the carriage disappeared down the passage.

"He almost looked real," he heard the girl say. "These rides are getting better all the time. Let's watch out for the maniac."

Mike made his way back along the track. He thought if he retraced his steps, there would be less chance of meeting up with his attacker.

He walked along the rails until he came up to the first cavern. He stopped dead. In front of him was another figure dressed like Frankenstein's monster, holding a large axe. He couldn't see the face because the body was facing away from him. Mike stood there keeping perfectly still.

I'm certain that wasn't there when I came in.

I'm positive. It must be him. He's changed costumes and he's waiting until I walk past before he grabs me.

Mike decided to take the initiative. I've nothing to lose, he thought, as he launched himself in a flying tackle at the threatening creature. The axe came flying out of the monster's hand and landed heavily, blade first on the ground, cutting through a power cable. The cave was plunged into darkness and the devilish noises around him groaned into silence. He struggled to his feet, completely disorientated. Suddenly, he felt a hand take hold of his collar and slowly tighten its grip round his neck.

He's going to strangle me, thought Mike. I'm going to die!

Chapter 20
SURPRISE SURPRISE

"Got you!" shouted a voice, which pierced through the pitch darkness.

Mike felt himself being hauled to his feet. He struggled like a wild animal, fearing that he was in mortal danger. The lights flickered back on as the emergency generator kicked in. Mike recognised the man who held his neck in a strangle hold, and stopped squirming when he realised it was the ride attendant.

"We've had enough of your kind in here!" he said, as he dragged Mike roughly towards the entrance. "Now clear off! If I see you round here again, I won't be so gentle next time!"

"Are you causing trouble again?" came a voice from behind. He turned round and saw Angela and Kate.

"What's happened to you?" asked Kate, concerned about the dried blood on his face. "I told you not to do anything stupid. Just look at you!"

Mike decided he'd had enough of the fairground. He wiped his face with a tissue that Kate gave him and brushed down his dirty clothes. "I'm going home," he said dejectedly. "I'll see you later on."

☠

Mike returned home feeling exhausted by his ordeal. "So much for plan B," he said, as he stretched out on the couch.

He reached over for his tape recorder and unplugged it from the phone. He took it over to the table and pressed the rewind button.

He started playing through all the threatening phone calls that he had received, hoping that he might recognise the voice or find a clue that he had missed before. Fifteen minutes later the tape had finished.

"Well, that was a complete waste of time," he said despondently, but he wasn't going to give up.

"I'll give it one more try." After rewinding the tape, he pressed the start button, and sat back to listen.

He put his feet up onto the table, closed his eyes and concentrated as he had never done before, catching every sound and noise on the tape.

Suddenly he jumped up. There was something he recognised and it wasn't the voice. He rewound it again and listened once more. He heard it again.

"I don't believe it! It's impossible, but it must be true! I know who's been making the phone calls and threatening my life!"

He grabbed his coat and ran out of the

house, stopping when he saw that Steve was coming up the garden path. "You're in a hurry," said Steve.

"Steve! I know who's responsible for the phone calls and the threats."

"You thought it was Rob Murray, didn't you?" asked Steve, concerned.

"No, it's not! I can't tell you yet! I've got to make sure I'm right! I'll see you later!" Mike ran off down the road leaving Steve to worry about what his friend had discovered.

☠

Ten minutes later Mike stopped, gasping for breath, outside Zilla's house. Anger was boiling up inside him.

"How could she do it?" he said, banging loudly with his fist on the front door. The curtains moved slightly and Mike could see Zilla's face peeping through.

"Mike," she said, as she opened the door. "Is there something wrong? You look terrible."

Mike pushed his way past her without saying a word. She followed him into the living room, watching as he paced up and down, clenching his fists and breathing heavily.

"Zilla - it was you! You're behind all the bizarre things that have been happening to me. I listened to a recording of all the phone calls and in the background I heard your cough. I knew then that it was you. Why did you do it?

You, of all people!" he bellowed, banging his fist down on the table.

Zilla blushed a bright red and tears began to fill her eyes. She put her hand over her face and her whole body shook as she began to sob violently.

"Why did you do it!" Mike repeated, not moved by the flood of tears.

Zilla looked up. Her eyes were bloodshot and filled with pain. "Mike, I'm sorry. I'm really sorry," she said, between sobs. "It was only meant to be a little game, but then it became more serious and I didn't know how to stop."

"There must have been someone else involved. It wasn't your voice on the tape, was it? Your coughing was in the background. Was it Rob Murray?"

"I can't tell you Mike! If he found out, he'd kill me! I'm frightened, Mike. He's dangerous!"

"You've got no choice!" he said, grabbing hold of her arm.

She paused for a moment then took a deep breath. "It was Steve. It was his idea in the first place."

Mike laughed coldly. "Don't try to be clever with me. Steve is my best friend. Why should he do anything to harm me?"

"He was jealous of you and Rachael, and when he found out that you were taking her out, he was determined to stop it. He wanted you out of the way."

"But why did you become involved?" asked

Mike, beginning to have doubts about Steve.

"Steve knew that I liked you, and he thought if his plan succeeded, he would finish up with Rachael and I would have you."

Mike shook his head.

"It seemed to be a laugh at first. I thought it was just a harmless prank, and I was very fond of you. I suppose I was jealous of Rachael. It was only later that I realised that Steve was obsessed with Rachael. When I found out what lengths he was prepared to go to, I became frightened and wanted to back out, but he wouldn't let me. He said I would be in trouble with the police and I didn't want you to know what I had been up to. Mike, I'm so ashamed." She looked up at Mike, hoping for some word of comfort.

Through the corner of her eye, Zilla saw a shadow pass by the doorway. She turned to see what it was. "Oh no! Please - no!" Her face froze in horror as she let out a piercing scream.

Chapter 21
MAD MAN

Mike turned quickly towards the door, but there was no one there.

"It was Steve! I saw him! He was listening! He must have heard everything that I said!"

"Where is he now?" asked Mike anxiously, as he walked into the hallway. There was no sign of anyone. He went into the kitchen, followed by Zilla.

"Look! He's in the garden," cried Zilla, pointing through the window. "He's going into the shed!"

"Why would he do that?" asked Mike, curiously. "Do you think he's trying to hide? I'm going to speak to him." He was about to open the kitchen door when Steve came out of the shed, carrying a huge claw hammer in his hand. He stopped and looked towards the window where Zilla and Mike were standing.

Mike swallowed hard. He had never seen Steve like this before. He started walking up the path towards the house. Zilla pushed past Mike and locked the door.

"He'll kill us! He's mad! You can't reason with him!"

Steve turned the handle trying to get in. The top half of the door was glass and Mike watched, mesmerized by the indistinct shape of a moving hammer which he could see through

140

the frosted glass.

The next moment, the glass flew in all directions as the hammer shattered the window pane. A hand reached through the broken window and turned the key in the lock. Mike remembered the terrifying nightmare he had had, but this was much worse. He stared into Steve's crazed eyes. This time, it was for real.

Zilla pulled Mike into the hallway. "We've got to get out of here," she shouted, as she attempted to open the front door. She soon realised that the deadlock was on and the key was missing.

Steve stood in the hallway holding the hammer in his white knuckled hand, while Mike and Zilla retreated into the living room.

"Steve - you need help!" Mike pleaded. "Let me phone the police before you make things worse for yourself."

He's like a deranged animal, he thought, as he looked into his eyes, which were glazed, staring right through him.

Steve stood there, his smile fixed into a horrible leer, as he twisted the hammer round and round in his hands. "So, you thought you could take Rachael away from me?" he hissed through his teeth. "We were made for each other."

"If you care so much about Rachael, how could you put her in danger? You must have cut the brakes on the car when you went back for your wallet. She could have been seriously injured," Mike explained, hoping that Steve would understand how stupid he had been. He soon realised that this was hopeless - Steve was beyond reason.

"If I can't have her, then no one can," he replied. A line of saliva came from the corner of his mouth and ran down his chin.

Mike moved across the room, frantically looking for something he could defend himself with. Steve lunged towards him and gave a wild swing with the hammer, but he was too far away.

He moved forward, getting closer, until he trapped Mike in the corner. He lashed out again at Mike's head, but Mike moved sideways and the hammer crashed into the wall, leaving a deep indent in the plaster.

Mike edged his way across to the other side of the room as Steve regained his balance. He came forward again with the hammer raised. Mike darted quickly out of the way as the hammer splintered the smooth surface of the wooden sideboard. He was desperate. "I can't keep on dodging these blows."

He looked at the open doorway thinking he could escape into the garden where he'd have more chance.

Steve must have seen Mike's glance because as he dashed for the opening, he kicked the door closed, trapping him as he tried to make his escape.

Steve grabbed Mike around the neck with

his free hand and dragged him into the centre of the room. Mike panicked. He tried to release himself from Steve's iron grasp but realising he wasn't strong enough, he prepared to make one last attempt to free himself before the hammer blow fell again.

Mike braced himself, then pushed forwards with all his might, sending them both lurching across the room towards two glass partition doors. The glass shattered as they both tumbled through. Fortunately for Mike, he was on top as they fell to the floor. The huge, jagged shards of glass from the door sliced into Steve's leg, severing the main artery as he hit the ground. A jet of blood shot up and splattered onto the white, artexed ceiling.

"Help me!" screamed Steve, as he began to drift into unconsciousness.

Horrified, Zilla ran to fetch a towel. Mike knelt down and pressed it firmly onto the wound to try and stem the flow of blood. "Phone the ambulance!" he shouted, as he cradled Steve in his arms.

Chapter 22
ZOMBIES TICKETS

Mike and Rachael sat together in a coffee bar. The memory of the horrific events of the last few weeks were now, thankfully, fading away.

"And I thought that Rob Murray was the culprit," mused Mike, as he stirred his coffee.

"I hope you apologised to him for all the trouble you caused. I thought he was a very nice person," said Rachael, smirking.

"Tell me the truth. Did you really like him?" asked Mike, feeling sorry for himself.

"I'm only pulling your leg," said Rachael, breaking into a radiant smile. "I've never stopped liking you."

"More than Rob Murray?"

"Of course."

"There's only one mystery that hasn't been solved," mused Mike. "Who sent those tickets for the Dead Zombies concert? That was what started the whole thing."

Rachael smiled coyly. "I did."

"You did?"

"I've liked you for a long time and I knew that you liked me. I also knew that you were shy and needed a bit of a push, so I thought I'd point you in the right direction."

Mike grinned. He knew he had been manipulated by this devious, clever female, but he didn't mind in the least.